THE
# FRIEND SHIP
ADVENTURE

Library of Congress Control Number
2020921571

ISBN
978-1-7360559-0-8

This is a first edition printing.

Storm Praise Publishing, LLC
Attn: Bruno's Friendship Chronicles
5668 Fishhawk Crossing Blvd.
Suite 130
Lithia, FL 33547

stormpraisepublishing@gmail.com

www.StormPraise.com

Copyright ©2021 by Carole G. Barton
Published by Storm Praise Publishing, L.L.C.

We love educators!

Visit the website below to request your free
teacher's guide.
https://snip.ly/cyd5sf

*In Loving Memory of My Mom*

# Chapter 1

When I close my eyes, I can still see the day when my great adventure began...

I stood with my hands on my hips in awe, at the top of the world, looking down at Somerset, England. I admired the amazing meadow through my black-framed goggles. The meadow was full of tall, green grass waving to all as it blew in the wind. The flowers were singing with delight at the beautiful day! I stared at the sun, bursting forth with yellow, pinkish-red, and purple colors as it peeked through the rain clouds. As I stared at the sky, I noticed a double rainbow that was looking right at me!

Standing on the top of the hill, I gazed down at the River Axe. It was not super-fast like a red squirrel, but it also wasn't as slow as a snail. I felt curious as I watched the water. I knew the river was full of fish. I heard that there were salmon, trout, and Kingfish in the river. I wanted to meet a King-fish to ask him how he kept his crown from falling off underwater!

I also wanted to see where the water was headed. I didn't know where it went, but as I attempted to follow the current through the water, I could faintly make out something past the meadow. I had never gone further than the meadow up until this point. I lived in the same place for my entire life. I watched people find treasures every day. It was my job. Some days there were marvelous items people left behind, like my circle pointer. On other days, I found absolutely nothing. I did enjoy getting to observe people. They were all so interesting in their unique ways.

I enjoyed the meadow, but ever since my buddy, Steve, moved away I couldn't stop dreaming of more. I wondered if the life I thought I saw beyond the meadow was worth exploring. I thought about what I would do and after about three seconds, I decided that it was time for a change.

I was going to go on a great exploration! I had no idea what was beyond the meadow, but I was determined to find out.

More than a grand adventure, the greatest treasure of all was to find a new friend. I needed someone to share my thoughts and ideas with, so I carefully climbed down the hill and went to my house to get ready for my journey. My house was not special in any way because it was just a roof over my head.

I grabbed my circle pointer as soon as I entered my home. I used it to know which direction to go in. I created a necklace out of rope and tied my circle pointer around my neck. I was certain that my circle pointer would find a way to a new friend!

I picked up my sturdy backpack and began to put supplies and tools inside of it for my adventure. I knew I needed food for my trip, so I packed my favorite food - CHEESE! I put an extra pair of black-framed goggles in my backpack because it is important to see exactly where you are going and where you have been. I wanted to be able to sleep peacefully so I also included my weighted blanket. It is important to get rest so that your body can do its best.

As I continued to pack, I saw my 'thinking stone'. It was beautiful! My 'thinking stone' looked as blue as the River Axe and I could see right through it! But most importantly, it was rough on one side and smooth on the other. I packed my 'thinking stone' because I hold it when I need to calm down and figure out the answers to problems.

I brought my comb with me so I could look nice for a new friend. I like the way it makes my head feel when I use it, too! I also brought my new magazine page. I like to look at faraway places. I looked at the strange writing on the page. Even though I didn't know what it said, I knew it must say something amazing. I packed food and tools that help me focus. I was ready for an adventure and dreamed of making a new friend.

As I slowly walked along, I had deep thoughts about meeting a new friend. I didn't have instructions or tools in my backpack for how to make a new friend. It was easy to start a friendship with my buddy, Steve, but that was a long time ago. If I found a new friend, I didn't know what to talk to him or her about! I walked and thought about what to do. I wanted to be prepared to talk to a new friend.

Let's see... I love to eat and my favorite food is cheese. I ate some cheese as I continued to think. I like to dream of faraway places. I enjoy good music. When I get a good beat going in my head, I feel relaxed. I started to hum and dance as I walked. I get into my music. I move my arms and legs to music and my heart feels the beat while my head moves back and forth. As I danced and walked, I also hoped to find a friend on my journey that likes some of the things I like.

I began to hum. Then I started skipping. I skipped faster and faster and faster. Before long, my feet got all caught up together and I went flying into the air! I felt like a bird. As I felt my body coming slowly back to the ground, I did a huge flip and landed on my gigantic feet perfectly! "I LANDED ON MY FEET! " I looked to the left. No one. I looked to the right. No one. I looked down at my feet with pride and said, " That was an impressive feat, feet!" I felt quite pleased with myself.

I wished someone saw my trick. I saw butterflies

fluttering by, but I could tell that they hadn't even noticed my trick. If they did, I knew they would have been impressed and spoke to me. I saw birds flying by, but they missed my big moment, too. They were probably on a mission to fly somewhere far away and wonderful. Bunnies were hopping by, but even they were too busy digging deep, deep holes to notice my super-cool flip.

I was watching the birds fly in the sky. CRASH! I had no idea that there was a hole right in front of me! I didn't see the big hole and I fell face-first into that deep dark tunnel!
OUCH!

As I brushed myself off, I poked my head out of the hole. My large, round, eyes looked around to see if anyone saw my mistake. I looked like a spy on an underground, secret mission. I  even heard spy music in my head!

I looked to the left. No one. I stopped and breathed a sigh of relief. I looked to my right and there in front of me was a sheep laughing his head off! As I stared at him, I saw his long hair in front of his big eyes. He was as puffy as a marshmallow!

I thought to myself, "REALLY?" Steve, my buddy that moved away, would have told me to keep on going and to make a new friend.

I could still hear the sheep laughing at me as I climbed out of the hole and walked away.

Have you ever noticed that when you do something awesome, there is no one around to see, not even a possum? But, when you fall, I mean really fall, there is always someone right there to see it all. It's like there is a speaker that shouts, "You gotta see this. Someone fell!" I haven't had a friend for a long time. Maybe one day, I could have one friend, just one.

I took my 'thinking stone' out of my backpack and thought about what happened. I did something amazing and no one saw it! I messed up and was laughed at by a sheep! I began to think about it. I was feeling anxious and a little embarrassed.

This was a small problem. When I say small, I mean tiny, like my nose. It was not a large problem (like my really big feet).

It certainly wasn't worth stopping my adventure. I kept going. I thought, "Oh well, maybe next time someone will see me do something amazing." I put my 'thinking stone' back in my backpack. While I was looking in my backpack, I took out more cheese to eat. I walked, ate, and skipped.

I checked my 'circle pointer' again. It was leading me straight ahead. I believed that a new friend would be on this path, too. I just had to walk, watch, and wait, but my feet were getting so tired. I felt like I was walking forever and I still had no idea what was beyond the meadow.

As the dandelions gently blew in the wind, I decided to take a break under the tall trees. I climbed up to the top of the rocks by the trail. I saw a spectacular view! The tall, green grass swayed back and forth as much as the wildflowers did. Through the gentle breeze, I heard the River Axe as it rushed by. It was even louder than when I started my trip. The sun was peeking at me through the tall trees all around me. The amazing glow was now straight up in the sky. I enjoyed the sounds and the wonders of the meadow. Before long, it was time for me to put my backpack back on and move on in my adventure. I couldn't decide if I should go fast or slow. I wasn't going to run, that was for sure! I don't think anyone would run with a backpack and a weighted blanket in it. It might be heavy, but it sure helped me focus and feel prepared for what came next. I just need to keep an eye out for any more holes!

As I walked along, I soon came to a lake. I slowed down to enjoy the view. I saw a swan gracefully swimming, all alone. I wanted to be polite and possibly make a new friend, so I quietly went over to the bank of the lake. As I stood there, I said clearly, "Good morning, swan! How are you today?" She didn't even say one word.

She stared at me for two seconds, proceeded to stare at my circle pointer, then opened her beak quite wide. I was so excited that she was going to

talk to me, but as I waited and watched, what I saw was strange. She wasn't able to make a sound! She just looked at me with sad eyes. I knew in my heart that she wanted to tell me something, but I didn't know what she was trying to say. I think she was attempting to speak to me in a silent language.

I said to her, "I noticed that you appreciate a good circle pointer."

After I said that the swan gracefully swam away with a tear falling down her cheek.

I thought back to what I said. I was polite to the

swan. Maybe she had something else to do or somewhere else to be. What I do know is that she did like my circle pointer. As I walked on, I heard a very loud bell ringing. While I didn't know where the swan had gone, I hoped that one day we could be friends.

As I walked on, I told myself, "You are on a mission. Your mission is to find a new friend beyond the meadow." With all of the new day still fresh in my brain, I began to skip again.

I decided to practice more flip tricks. I started skipping very quickly this time. But it felt different for some reason. I wasn't sure why. Before I could figure out what was different, my body was coming off the ground again! I was mid-air and turning upside down when I could feel my huge feet get tangled up in a big mess. I was certain that this would not turn out well. I held onto the air for as long as I could and then, THUD! My body dropped to the ground.

"OUCH" I shouted as I landed on the earth.

I opened my eyes and the first thing I saw was a hedgehog staring right back at me. My heart began to beat faster. My face was red and glowing. I was so embarrassed.

I wanted to at least try to talk to the hedgehog, but I never knew for sure where a hedgehog's ears could be found. They have so many spikes! Were his ears on his nose? Were they on his back? Then, it dawned on me! His ears must be on his belly button!

I got down low to the ground and loudly spoke into his tummy, "GOOD MORNING, HEDGEHOG!

HOW ARE YOU?" The hedgehog curled up into a ball.

I looked down at my enormous feet. Like my flip in front of him, my first time meeting the hedgehog had fallen flat.

As I walked away, I started to wonder if there was something wrong with me. I tried to become friends with a swan and a hedgehog and both of them didn't want to have anything to do with me.

I walked with my head down, feeling sorry for myself when I came to a very large puddle in the meadow. I looked down into the water. My black-framed goggles were falling down my face. I adjusted my goggles. I already ate a great deal of cheese during all of my snack breaks. I wiped my mouth. My hair was everywhere from all of the flips I had done that day. I took my comb out of my backpack so I could fix my hair. I looked back into the puddle one more time. I said to my reflection, "Hello, how are you today?" I chuckled as I continued, "I'm well, how are you?" I need to remember that I have always liked me. I smiled as I walked on.

As I kept walking on and on, I started feeling my small problem grow from nose size to foot size. I began to think that making a new friend was a big problem. I knew that I needed to use my tools to fight my thoughts of giving up. I didn't want to get stuck and I didn't want my brain to stop growing.

I found a place to sit in the meadow. I opened my backpack and took my weighted blanket out. I stretched out in the tall grass, put the blanket around myself, and looked up at the sky. The feeling of the weights in the blanket helped me shake off my negative thoughts. I just kept on thinking and saying to myself, "I can find a new friend." The more I said this, the happier I felt. I took a deep breath and held it for seven seconds. I let that deep breath out and continued to tell myself, "I can do this." While I was taking a break, I took more cheese out of my backpack. For me, it's good to have a snack when I'm feeling hungry.

I took my thinking stone out of my backpack. I held it my hand. I stood there for a moment and then, I started to do some stretches. Stretching your body is just as important as stretching your brain. As I stretched, I started to sing and of course, I had to dance, too. As I moved my arms and legs through the air in a jerking way, I wondered if anyone might be watching me.

I put my tools in my backpack. I checked my circle pointer to make sure I was going in the right direction, and then I stretched one last time. I decided to walk slowly as I thought deep thoughts. Using my tools has helped my brain grow and change. I used to think only negative thoughts, but now I have replaced them with positive thoughts. With confidence, I said aloud to the air, "This may take some time and some effort, but I've got this!"

# Chapter 2

I heard people talking so I stopped to listen closer. I love people watching. This reminded me of all of the people watching I did in the meadow. I heard a very deep and strong English accent asking, "Do you think we can travel deeper next time?"

Then a high pitched voice next to him answered back. "I think we may have found a way to go deeper. We just need to bring extra equipment," she said.

I stared at the people, wondering what they could've been talking about. I wondered where they were going and why they were dressed alike. I studied the outfits they were wearing. They wore shiny, black suits with strange-looking treasures around their waists. I thought to myself, "Maybe they carry their tools around their waists and not their backs the way I do."

I heard laughing. Then another man said, "We need more boats, long-lasting flashlights, more oxygen tanks, and more clips to go through there and I'm sure that I'll be carrying everything, again!" He kept on laughing.

Still not knowing what they were talking about, I looked at another man dressed in the same shiny, black suit. He was walking with the group, but he wasn't part of the group. None of the other people talked with him and he didn't talk with the other people. It looked like the man was talking to the trees and the birds flying by. He was reading a book aloud, repeating himself a lot. Before I knew it, he was looking right at me! I froze. I didn't know what to do. I didn't want to mess things up because I thought this man could be a good friend for me. I decided to speak softly and then wait for him to respond to me. I cleared my throat. I gently said, "Hello sir, my name is Bruno. How are you today?" I stared at him, waiting for his response.

He gently closed the book that he was telling the trees all about. He held the book closely, moved his eye gaze down to me and then, he looked at me! My heart started to beat faster as I waited for him to talk to me. The man calmly replied, "Hello Bruno. My name is Bill."

I was so happy! My head started spinning with ideas of what to say next but, before I had a chance to speak, the other people in the shiny, black suits started talking to Bill. "Who are you talking to Bill?" They looked right down at me in the tall, green grass. Then they stated, "There is no one here. We are almost at Wookey Hole. Look, there's your bat friend, waiting for you." Then the three people with Bill started to laugh.

Bill quickly looked up and said, "I see Wookey Hole. I see AVA. AVA is my friend." Bill walked away from me as he made his way toward his friend.

He didn't even say goodbye to me. I began to feel a knot in my stomach. At first, my heart was so happy and now it felt empty all over again. It reminded me of when I met the swan and the hedgehog. My brain was starting to get stuck. I took a deep breath in and out.

I also started thinking about Bill. The other shiny black suit people didn't seem like they were friends with Bill and because of that, I was glad that Bill had a friend in Ava. I hoped that one day I might be lucky enough to see Bill again. I hoped we could be friends, too.

As I walked on feeling calmer, I could see the meadow start to change. I walked for a very long time. The tall, green grass was getting shorter and shorter. As I came to the end of the meadow, I wondered if I had gone too far. I stopped and stared at the short grass in front of me. I turned around and through my black-framed goggles, I could see how far I had come that day. I hadn't left a cheese trail to find my way back home. I couldn't turn back. I stood still, unsure of what to do.

While I was standing and thinking, I heard a faint noise. It sounded like a voice. I couldn't help but follow it. I had to know whose voice it was. As I got closer, the voice became clearer. I heard laughter and singing. I hoped with all my heart that this person liked music, dancing, and talking as much as I do!

# Chapter 3

I dared to dream that this person wouldn't mind me dropping in unannounced.

"GR-Gr-Gr" my stomach grumbled loudly. I looked into my backpack for something to eat. I ate all my cheese! I was verrrrrrry hungry and I had no more food to eat. I took another deep breath in. I held that breath for seven seconds and then I let that deep breath out. I was hopeful that the person whose voice I heard would have some food to share with me.

The meadow stopped. The shorter grass was gone.

I came to a clearing and saw her for the first time. It was a lady kneeling in the dirt. She had lots of flowers everywhere. As I got a little closer, I could hear her talking to her plants. She laughed as she said, "Here you go, little flower. I hope you like a little water with your dirt."

I wanted to make a good impression. I came so far and I hadn't made a new friend yet. I also had questions about the strange group of people I saw. I knew nothing about this Wookey Hole place they were talking about.

As my thoughts began to spin around in my head, I took another deep breath in. I held it for seven seconds and then I let that deep breath out. I made sure my goggles were on just right and then I straightened my backpack.

Here I go again! "Hello, my name is Bruno. How are you today?"

I waited for, what felt like forever, for her to respond. She looked down at me. The lady had big blue eyes and her face had a great big smile on it. "Hello Bruno. My name is Virginia. I'm doing well. How are you?"

My heart was beating out of my chest! She spoke to me and she wanted to know how I was doing! This is what I was waiting for all day long!

"Hello," I chuckled. "Would you say your name again? I didn't quite hear it?"

I said her name over and over again. Each time I got it wrong, she would laugh with me, not at me, and say, "It's okay, Bruno.  Just keep trying." She was so nice to me. I tried again, "Is your name Big G yuh?"

With her big blue eyes and her amazing smile, she stared at me while she thought. Then she replied, "Bruno, why don't you come up with a nickname for me? Does that sound like a good idea?"

"It sure does! Wait, what is a nickname?" I asked.

She said with kindness and understanding in her voice, "A nickname is a name you use to talk with someone. It can be a name that describes them in some way. It is usually a short name that is easier to say than their real name."

I thought and thought until I came up with a perfect nickname. "You are the sweetest lady I have ever met. May I call you Lady?"

"That sounds good to me," Lady said.

We talked and talked and talked. I told her the reason for my journey. I showed her my backpack and told her all about my tools. I explained each tool and what I use it for. She looked at everything carefully.

She saw the circle pointer that I wore around my neck. As she took a closer look, she noticed that the arrow inside didn't move.

Lady looked at my comb, weighted blanket, and the thinking stone. After taking all the information in, Lady stated, "Bruno, I am so happy that you know what tools to use to help yourself focus and feel better. This is a big deal and so important.

I smiled as my heart jumped with joy. She complimented me and it was my first compliment ever!

I replied,"Thank you," ever so quietly.

Lady then saw Bruno's torn magazine page. Lady said in amazement, "Wow, Bruno, I haven't been there in a long time."

"Where Lady?" I asked.

"Well, to Wookey Hole. See it says it right here."
She pointed to the writing as she looked at Bruno.

"You know what that says?" I was hardly able
to contain my excitement! Lady was so nice and
intelligent.

I also wondered where I heard Wookey Hole
before, but it was not the time to daydream. I
needed to hear what Lady had to say.

Lady smiled at me and kindly responded, "Bruno,
I used to teach elementary school. I taught my
students how to read. Would you like to learn how
to read?"

"Oh, yes, please," I said. "That would be amazing!"

"Great, we can start by learning and singing the
alphabet," Lady was so delighted. It had been so
long since Lady worked with a student!

We worked on the ABC's over and over again. Lady would draw a letter in the dirt and then I would draw it. I'm not very good at drawing, which is why I preferred singing the alphabet. We sang the ABC's a lot. I knew all the letters, as long as Lady sang with me.

Then Lady spoke to me about how all the letters make sounds. She also told me that when you put them together in different ways, they make words. I was on my way to learning how to read!

The first word that Lady taught me was cat, 'C-A-T'.

Now, I knew that I was a numbers guy, so I started counting to show Lady. "One, four, three, six, thirty-seven." I counted all by myself.

I asked Lady a reading and number question. "How many words are there?"

She thought for a while. "There is no way to know how many words there are because new words are added all the time. The number is always growing." I thought that was interesting!

As the day went by, I took my black-framed goggles off. I said as I rubbed my eyes, "Is it okay if we stop reading and writing for today, Lady?"

"That sounds like a great idea. You did so much today and hiked so far that your body is tired. Your brain was also stretched so much from learning how to read and write. Why don't you watch me plant flowers? We could listen to music if you like," Lady said as she looked at her new visitor.

I nodded with a big smile. This turned out to be a great day! Lady turned on a machine that had music coming out of it. The music was slow. Lady started to dance and sing.

I asked Lady, "What is that machine?"

Lady said, "That machine is my phone. It can do a lot of different things, but one of my favorite things it can do is to play music. I can show you how to use it. Would you like that?"

"That would be great! I love music and dancing, too." I was so excited! We both love to talk. We both like music and dancing. I'm glad that friends can have things in common. This day was getting better and better.

I listened to Lady's music that was playing on her phone. It was slow and I didn't understand what the voices were saying.

I said with a question in my voice, "What is this called?"

"This type of music is called opera," Lady said.

Lady closed her eyes as she got lost in the music.

I thought maybe I should give it a try. I closed my eyes, too. The music was slow at first. Then, it began to get louder and louder. The pitch was frightening! I kept on trying to like the music for Lady. Then the music got super soft and a bit spooky. Before long, I was curled up like the hedgehog in the meadow. I heard something scrEEEEEEECH!!!!! I couldn't take it anymore, "MAKE THE OPERA, STOP-era!"

Lady burst into laughter and paused the song.

"Oh, Bruno, that's the teakettle!"

I politely asked Lady if I could change the music. She nodded yes and showed me how to do it myself.

Soon after I changed the music, I heard my kind of beat. It was a strong beat that is great to dance to.

I turned the music louder so Lady could enjoy the good music, too.

I did all my best dance moves. I moved my arms to my side and then up in the air. I moved my head back and forth. I moved my feet all around. For a moment, I thought I was going to get all twisted up! Good thing my fancy foot-work kept going, because Lady could not stop staring at what a great dancer I am! I'm sure I am the best dancer she has ever seen!

I don't think she liked my music at first. What I do know is that she loved my dancing. We both started singing and dancing to very fast music. After the song was over and we clapped, Lady told me that she took dance classes three times a week. I think with a little more practice, her dancing could be as cheesy as mine.

Since Lady doesn't like my music the best, we took turns listening to each others' music. Lady and I are the same and different and that's one thing I like about our new friendship.

Lady said, "I'm all done with planting, teaching, listening, and dancing for today. I have to wash up. Would you like to have lunch with me in the garden?"

As soon as she mentioned there would be lunch, I could barely stop myself from doing a super cool-flip for her. We were so busy talking, learning how to read, enjoying music, and dancing that I forgot how hungry I was when I met Lady. I said, "Yes, please and thank you! May I help you with it?"

Lady smiled and replied in a very cool voice, "I've got this. Go ahead and look around the backyard. I will be right back."

And with that, she headed quickly into her beautiful thatched roof house. Her house was as white as the clouds in the sky. I'm sure the inside of her house was just as cheerful as she is.

As I looked around, there were gorgeous flowers all around the house. I turned and saw a green hedge that enclosed Lady's wonderful yard. As I took a closer look at the types of flowers, I saw a bluish-purple lavender plant that smelled amazing! There were red and yellow roses all around the garden. There was also a beautiful purple tree in the center of the garden. Butterflies fluttered all around the tree. Hummingbirds whistled happily in the backyard. Life was full of color and wonder in the garden. I looked at Lady through the kitchen window as she smiled and waved at me.

When Lady came back to the garden with food, I couldn't believe my eyes! She had so much food and I was so very hungry! I was feeling excited. I took a deep breath again. I held it for the usual seven seconds and then I let that deep breath out. I was so hungry, but I remembered my manners and waited for Lady.

I smiled a big smile and then my eyes got smaller and smaller. This was not my usual face.

When she saw my face, she became worried. Lady said, "Do you like cheese? I assumed that you like cheese because you are a mouse. If you don't like cheese, I could make something else. Do you want me to make something else?"

"Oh, it is perfect. I'm just really hungry," I responded. As Lady reached for food, I did too. We both ate and ate. As Lady drank her tea, I shared, "I ate cheese before, but I never had this kind of cheese. It has a different flavor."

Lady smiled and said, "It came from Wookey Hole. There's a room of the cave that is full of cheese. It is kept there for a long time. It is called Wookey Hole

Cheddar Cheese and it's famous all over England and beyond. Do you like it?"

"WOW!" I exclaimed, " I never ate Wookey Hole Cheddar Cheese. It is the best cheese that I have ever eaten! May I have more, please?" My stomach was feeling better, but I couldn't figure out where I heard that name Wookey Hole before. I knew I heard it, but I just couldn't figure out when I heard it.

Happily, Lady nodded and gave me more cheese. She also looked at me with a grin. "I grow fruit in my garden. I always have strawberries with my cheese sandwiches. Would you like to try some?"

Having never tried a strawberry before, I was eager to try Lady's suggestion. I put a great, big, red berry on top of my cheese sandwich. Just before I went to bite my sandwich, the strawberry decided it wanted to go on an adventure, too! The round, red fruit rolled down the garden, into the clearing, and back to the meadow. I raced after it with my enormous feet pounding the ground as fast as I could go! Lady was yelling at me, "Let it go, I have more!"

I was determined to catch this runaway fruit. As I was catching up to it, I could hear the sheep laughing and cheering for the strawberry to win the race! Much to my surprise and the sheep's surprise, I captured the strawberry! Before I had time to catch my breath, I saw the people in the shiny black suits again. This time, I didn't stop and stare. Then I heard a gentle voice say, "Hi, Bruno." I turned to find out that it was Bill talking.

"Hi Bill," I replied. The people funnily looked at Bill. It wasn't the laughter, type of funny. They stared at Bill and then looked down in the tall, green grass, right at me, and then back at Bill. The man with the deep, strong English accent said, "Bill, who are you talking to?"

The high pitched voice stated, "Bill your bat friend is at Wookey Hole. There is no one here."

Bill's eyes shifted down to the ground. I was feeling bad for Bill, so I stated in a very clear voice, "Bill, tell Ava I said hi, okay?" Bill looked at me and smiled with his big dark eyes.

It was that exact moment when I realized where I heard the name Wookey Hole! I remembered the shiny, black suit people talking about it. Lady also said it was the place in the photo on my magazine page.

I raced back to ask Lady about this Wookey Hole place and the people in the shiny, black suits.

Out of breath, I said before the words would leave me again, "Lady, I've got to know now..."

"Bruno, are you okay? Lady said with a worried look on her face, "You were gone for a while. Did you catch the strawberry?"

"I forgot about the strawberry. I saw some people that I'm curious about. I was hoping you might know about them," as I slowly caught my breath.

"Who are the people that wear the strange black, shiny suits that I saw? They walk through the meadow going to someplace called WOO-something?"

# Chapter 4

As Lady smiled, her whole face sparkled. "Why, yes Bruno. I do know who you are talking about. Let's go sit and swing so I can tell you all about them."

So, we walked over to the wooden swing that was tied to an old tree with rope. We started swinging back and forth together.

"The people you are talking about are called cavers. They wear diving suits. The outfits keep them warm in the freezing water. A lot of caves around here, such as Wookey Hole, have underwater parts."

I thought about it and it made sense, but I needed to find out so much more.

"Lady, you mentioned Wookey Hole," I paused for a moment. "Since I know that Wookey Hole is a cave, is it a little cave or a gigantic cave?"

Lady stated, "If they had all the surrounding caves connected, Wookey Hole would be one of the largest cave system, but for now most of it is underwater. Remember? That is why the cavers need wetsuits."

"Thank you for telling me," I said trying hard to remember my manners. I'm a curious fellow." I was hoping that Lady would understand.

As Lady continued to swing slowly back and forth with me she replied, "Bruno, knowledge is so important. You need to ask questions so your brain can continue to grow and so you can learn more and more. Do you have any other questions?"

I thought some more and then I asked my best question yet. "Why do people go caving?"

Lady smiled and thought for a while. "I think that people go caving because they want to find out what lies beyond. With Wookey Hole, cavers may one day be able to connect all the cave systems in Somerset, England. I think that it would be amazing." Lady looked just like I do when I daydream.

All of a sudden, Lady stopped swinging back and forth and looked right at me. With her big, blue eyes sparkling at me, she asked me, "Did I tell you why Wookey Hole is so important to me?"

I shook my head no and waited for her answer. I started to wonder if she had gone caving before.

"When I was a little girl, my family and I would go to Wookey Hole every summer. My grandfather was a caver and he wanted me to follow in his footsteps. He even taught me how to swim in the pool at Wookey Hole. He took me on the tour to see the Wookey Witch." Her eye gaze shifted in my direction. I was hiding under a rock and shaking.

"Don't worry, Bruno. The Wookey Witch is a rock in the cave! There have been a lot of stories made up about it as time has passed," said Lady as she chuckled.

I quickly got out from under the rock. I stared at Lady as she went on with the story.

Lady went back to telling me her story of Wookey Hole. "My grandfather would explain the different rock formations. The water that drips down and falls to the floor helps to make rock formations called stalactites."

"Sta-what-a what-a?" I was a confused mouse.

Lady paused for a moment and then grew a great big smile on her face. "Bruno, my grandfather and I would go on the tour to see and smell the famous Wookey Hole Cheddar Cheese." She saw me sitting, staring right back at her with a big grin.

"My family and I would go camping at Wookey Hole, too." Lady looked as if she was dreaming again as she continued to share. "We would sing songs and sit by the campfire and count the stars."

I knew Lady was daydreaming because it was still day time and it looked like she was trying to count stars!

She continued to tell her story, "During the day, my brothers and I would climb rocks with our grandfather as we pretended to be great cavers. We would see who could climb the highest." As I watched her slipping back into another dream, I smiled. This was a good dream. I loved hearing all about it. I was starting to dream, too.

I wondered why no one else was home with Lady, so I politely asked, "Where are all the people now?"

She looked a little sad as she said, "This is my family's farm and I am the last member to live here. It gets lonely here sometimes, but I do have my flowers to talk to. And now I have you to talk to, as well." She smiled at me. Lady took a deep breath in and out. She shared a thought with me, "I have a great idea. Since I am helping you learn how to read and write, why not stay here in my little thatched roof house? I know it isn't much and I know you have your own house in the meadow, but I could sure use the company. You can help me with the flowers and I will help you read and write. What do you think?" Lady hoped that I would stay.

I thought for only three seconds when I eagerly said, "I think, YES! Yes, please, and thank you!"

I didn't tell Lady, but I was lonely, too. I needed someone to talk to. I was happy to learn how to read and write, I wanted to learn more about faraway places, but, best of all, I found Lady. She is a true friend. As I thought more and more about it, I got all choked up inside.

When everything settled, I followed her into the house. She escorted me from one room to another. They were huge rooms!

When we reached the kitchen, Lady smiled and said, "I have a great idea! Let's make popcorn. We can melt Wookey Hole Cheddar Cheese on top. What do you think, Bruno?"

I jumped for joy! That sounded amazing to me! As I nodded yes, Lady smiled and put some popcorn in the microwave. We kept talking as the popcorn popped. Lady melted the cheese on the stove and I watched from a distance.

After the cheese and popcorn cooled off, Lady gave me my very own bowl. She poured popcorn in and then carefully dripped melted cheese all over it. My eyes grew bigger and BIGGER until I couldn't wait any longer! I plunged my head right into the ooey-gooey goodness! My furry face was covered with ooey-gooey goodness! I smiled at Lady as cheese dripped off my nose. It wasn't long before I was so full that I thought I would burst!

I stopped eating for a while to look around Lady's kitchen. I was so into the food that I forgot to take a look around before we ate. I noticed something strange on Lady's counter. I walked over to take a closer look. It smelled different. There was no cheese on it. Something had to be wrong. "Lady, what is this?" I asked with a concerned look on my face.

"Oh, I'm making that for tomorrow. It is called Toad in a Hole," Lady said in between bites of ooey-gooey goodness.

I know what it is like to be inside a hole, but I cannot imagine not being able to move inside a hole! I had to help this poor toad! I climbed up on top of the hole and started screaming, "I'm here to help, Toad. Just hold on!" I kept looking for a way to get in, but it was all dark! Then, I heard Lady laughing. I turned and asked in a curious voice, "What's so funny?"

Lady kept laughing and gently said, "Toad in the Hole is English sausage in Yorkshire pudding. The Yorkshire pudding is pancake mix without sugar. There is no Toad inside. No toad was harmed in the making of this dish."

I was still weirded out by the name of the dish so I made a strange face at her. Lady saw how uncomfortable I was, so she kindly asked, "Would you like me to put Wookey Cheddar Cheese inside the Yorkshire pudding?" I thought for three seconds and then with a big grin, I laughed and said, "TOAD-ALLY!" Lady laughed a big belly laugh.

After Lady showed me around the kitchen we went into the Great Room. I knew why it had that name. There were pictures on the walls of so many people doing all kinds of great things. I saw pictures of people eating ice cream, climbing hills, and even a picture of people at Wookey Hole! Lady told me all about the people in the pictures. She was so happy to share her feelings about the pictures with me!

When Lady saw me yawn, she told me it was time for bed. I followed her to the table by the big window in the Great Room. I looked out the window at all of the flowers looking back at me. Then, Lady took out her shiny, metal jewelry box. It was silver and very strong. It had a red velvet pillow inside. She carefully took her jewelry out of the box and carefully placed it in the middle of the table. Lady said this would be my new bed!

With my weighted blanket, I climbed into bed. It was a perfect fit for me, except for my enormous feet that hung over the edge. Lady said, "Bruno your feet aren't that big, but for your comfort, I will help you." Lady fixed this by putting a book about Wookey Hole under my feet. She said, "There you go Bruno, now you can even dream about Wookey Hole. Tomorrow, when you wake up, you can look at the pictures."

I wanted to talk more with Lady, but as the sun was going down, so were my eyelids. I took off my goggles and put them by my bed. Lady tucked me in and then started singing one of her favorite songs. I think it was the opera stuff that I didn't understand, but this time, I didn't want to turn it off. I kept watching Lady's smiling face and big blue eyes as my eyelids got heavier and heavier.

With my eyes closed, I remembered the hillside and the start of the day. In my head, I replayed all the things that had happened along the way. I did a super cool flip and I fell into a gigantic hole. I was not able to make friends with the swan or the hedgehog, yet, but I did meet Bill. As I began to doze off, I thought about how wonderful it was to have met Lady. "My adventure has just begun," I whispered to myself as I drifted off to sleep.

## Chapter 5

As I lay there in the best bed I ever had, I looked out at the sun rising to greet me, just as it does, every day. This morning the sun looked brighter through the trees as if it were smiling at me. I smiled back at the sun and waved. Then, I began to think about how happy I was to have met Lady.

From the first time I saw her taking care of her plants, I knew she was nice. She was talking to plants that couldn't talk back to her. When she turned around, I saw her sparkling blue eyes. She even smiled when she spoke to me! Lady has the greatest laugh that I have ever heard in my life!

It starts small and builds to a waterfall of laughs. When I hear it, it makes me laugh!

I smiled as I thought of Lady. I could hear her singing to herself in my mind. I wanted to stay with her forever. Lady and I have a lot in common, I thought. We like talking, music, and dancing. We both have tools. I use my tools to help me focus. I have my weighted blanket that helps calm me when I need it. I have my thinking stone that helps me problem solve. I have my circle pointer because I never know if I am going to need help finding something. I knew it worked. After all, it did lead me right to Lady. Then, I started thinking about Lady's tools. She has a lot. She has gardening tools that help her have the most beautiful flowers in all of England! Inside her house, she has cooking tools that help her make the best food, ever! She has other stuff in her thatched roof house, I'm sure of it!

As I continued to smile, I wondered where she

was and what we would do on this beautiful day. I did my morning stretches so my brain and my body would be ready to take on whatever the day threw at me. As I looked up at the day, I said, "just kidding." I do like a good game of catch, but don't throw anything too hard today, okay?

I got up out of my bed. I folded the corners and fluffed the pillows. It looked just like Lady showed me the night before. I know because I took a brain picture of it. I put my weighted blanket inside my backpack, put my backpack on, and moved it around on my back until the weights felt just right.

I could hear noise coming from the kitchen. I went to find out what was happening. It was Lady making food! I stretched one more time and said, "Good morning, Lady, what's for breakfast?" I continued to sniff the amazing smells as I waited for her answer.

"Good morning, Bruno. We are having a proper

English breakfast; fried tomatoes, bacon, eggs, and toast. Doesn't that sound like a great way to start the day?" Lady was waiting for my answer. It sounded like a lot of food. I never heard of some of the foods she mentioned. With a puzzled look on my face, I shook my head from left to right. I didn't want a proper English breakfast.

Lady looked at my face and quickly changed the menu. "Bruno, have you ever tried Welsh Rarebit?"

I stared at Lady, still confused.

Lady smiled the biggest smile. "You will love it, I know it. It is made with melted Wookey Hole Cheddar Cheese and toasted bread."

I smiled big this time! I nodded in agreement so quickly I thought my head would fall off! We both laughed hard. Lady and I ate and talked and talked. After breakfast, Lady cleaned up and put away everything she took out. Everything in Lady's house had a place. I liked that. I wished that maybe one day, I would have a place in her home, too.

Lady pulled ABC letter cards out of her pocket. It looked like it was school time. Lady had big news to share. "Bruno, I have some work that I need to do in my hobby room, so I am going to have you trace over your ABC's with these cards today." I looked at the cards. The papers had dots all over them and under the dots were letters. I liked the ABC cards. Lady has some neat stuff in her house!

After sharing her big news, Lady asked me something strange. "Can I use this pencil and paper to trace around your body, Bruno?" I thought about it. Lady was always doing nice things for me, so I smiled and answered, "Sure, but may I do one thing, too?"

"Of course, what do you need?"

"I want to trace your hand," I looked up at her and through my goggles and tried to look patient, but it was super hard to wait for her answer.

"Of course, you can Bruno, but why do you want to trace my hand," Lady asked as she looked at me with a question on her face. I could feel my heart beating faster. I started getting hot. I even felt a lump in my throat. How would I tell her? I took my usual seven second breath in and out and then I slowly opened my mouth.

"So, wherever I go or whatever I do, I can always hold your hand," I told her.

She nodded, smiled, and looked at me as if she was taking a brain picture. Lady made me lay down on the kitchen counter to trace around my body. The pencil tickled as it touched my fur. We both laughed.

Then it was my turn. She gave me a smaller pencil to hold in both of my hands. It took some time, but I got all around her whole hand. Lady helped me fold the paper up so I could put it in my backpack. I wanted to put it in there so I could have a reminder of Lady with me always.

Lady told me she had a secret project in the hobby room that she had to finish.

I am not a big fan of secrets. I like to know what is coming. I knew if I was going to find out what was going on in the hobby room, I needed a lot of different skills. I needed my goggles so I could see every clue that I found. I would use my thinking stone to help me come up with good ideas. And I couldn't forget my circle pointer! I needed it to show me the best way to get to the hobby room.

Lady really wanted to surprise me, but I just had to take a peek. I decided to start dusting. It would make sense for me to move from the kitchen and down the hall to the hobby room if I was dusting. She was in her hobby room with the door closed. I had to know! I needed to come up with a plan to peek under the door or go outside and look through the window. As I thought and thought about what to do, it started... I could hear her opera music! "I yelled out loud to myself, "Scrap the mission!" Over and out!"

I sat down in the kitchen and traced the letters, just as Lady taught me. When I finished tracing the letters, I decided to take a walk outside to enjoy the beauty of the garden. The roses gave off such a spectacular smell! It was like nothing I ever smelled before. It smelled even better today than yesterday! I don't know how that was possible, but I enjoyed it anyway.

As I sat on Lady's swing with the wind gently moving it back and forth, the cavers came walking by. I knew who they were and where they were headed. I looked at the cavers with new eyes. I also focused on the tools around their waists.

Lady said they used tools that help them climb up the cave walls, like axes. They also have special tools to dive down into the cave water. I thought of the tools in my backpack that I use to help me climb out of negative moods. I smiled as I held the straps of my backpack a little tighter than usual.

"Hi," said a familiar voice. I looked over to see Bill come to a halt, looking right at me. But, nothing changed with the other cavers. They walked up to Bill and said, "Bill, we have to get going. No stopping now." Bill looked down and began to walk. I yelled, "I'll see you later, Bill." He turned around and smiled at me.

I started wondering more and more about what Lady told me about Wookey Hole. It sounded like a wonderful and amazing place. I hoped Bill would have a good day there. I knew I was going to have a great day. I smelled the flowers, heard Lady's music, and thought about Lady's secret project. If I couldn't get closer to see, at least I could guess what it might be!

I thought Lady might be working on a new backpack for me.

I never owned shoes before. I wondered if the surprise was sneakers that could help me jump higher. Then I thought maybe it was earmuffs! I liked that idea because I wouldn't hear as much of Lady's opera!

I wondered if any of my guesses were right. I wouldn't know until Lady was done. I thought it was a good idea to work in the garden so I could keep my mind off the secret. It was also a beautiful day in the backyard and I promised Lady I would help her take care of her flowers if she taught me how to read. I started pulling at weeds. Lady made it look like it was easy, but it was actually very hard work! I decided to use my teeth. That made me very proud of my really sharp teeth! They took care of those weeds in no time!

Then, I had to, one by one, carry those weeds to the bucket. I didn't understand why Lady didn't want to plant weeds because they tasted good to me. I wondered if it was a good idea to talk to Lady about planting some weeds beside her strawberries.

My stomach started to rumble. Thankfully, Lady packed a cheese sandwich for me so I could have another picnic in the backyard. I love picnics. I ate and ate until I couldn't eat another bite. When I was done, I put everything back into my backpack. The wind was blowing softly causing the flowers to sway. I started getting my kind of music stuck in my head. I had no choice. I had to get up and dance.

I did some of my great dance moves. Lady wasn't there to be my dance partner. I looked around and saw a beautiful rose standing there so I started to dance with it. Everything was going well until I took the lead. Something bad happened. The rose stuck me with its thorns! Thank God, I have a lot of fur or it could have been very painful! I have to remember that roses don't make good dance partners! If they don't get to lead, they will hurt you with their thorns!

"Not nice, rose! Not nice!" I said to the thorny flower. As the cavers walked by the garden that afternoon, Bill looked over to see me jumping up and down in front of the rose. I was still upset with the rose. I stopped and waved at Bill. Bill waved back and it wasn't long until the other cavers started all over again, saying that there was no one there. That seemed to make Bill feel sad. That made me look forward to a day when Bill and I could show the other cavers that Bill was not talking to the air and that I was there talking with him. Until then, I knew that Bill knew I was there and that is all that mattered to me.

I hadn't realized that I was in the garden all day until the cavers walked by! Lady was in her hobby room all day making something. I had no idea what she was up to, but I still wasn't going near that room with opera still playing!

Soon after I finished my cool dance moves in the backyard, I went back to work on the flowers. Lady's opera music stopped! That made me smile with relief. It was so quiet that I could hear the wind flowing through the trees and the birds singing in the meadow.

Lady came out of the house. She was smiling, carrying something in her hands. It was some sort of box. She put it down in front of me and said, "Bruno, I made something special, just for you. Go ahead, open the box," Lady said.

# Chapter 6

I had never received a present before! I stared
at the box so I could take the moment in. I took
another brain picture. The brown box that was in
front of me was tied up with a yellow ribbon. The
bright yellow ribbon reminded me of the sun shining
down on me when I traveled through the meadow
and met Lady. I looked at Lady's face. She was so
excited. Her hands were folded and ready to clap
for me. She worked all day on what was inside
the box. I knew before I even opened it that I was
going to love whatever it was because it was made
by Lady with care. I removed the yellow ribbon and
twisted it up. I knew it might come in handy in case I

ever needed some rope to climb with, just like cavers do. I looked at Lady, hopping up and down in excitement. As I opened the lid and jumped for joy! I pulled out the coolest black shiny wet suit ever! I quickly took my backpack off and put the wetsuit on. It was just my size!

"That is why I needed you lay on the paper this morning. I traced you so I could make the suit your exact size," Lady said.

I nodded and grinned. I looked up at Lady and proudly said, "I look like a caver." When I thought it wasn't possible, Lady made the gift even better!

She squealed, "There's more. Look inside the box!"

"There's more than this? What could it be?" I said to Lady.

I looked back into the box. Inside was a round, clear

helmet. I slowly pulled it out. I held it in my hands because it was so special. I looked at Lady so she could tell me more about it.

"This is the small-scale model of the large helmet my grandfather wore when he went caving at Wookey Hole. It was in the great room. I keep it in a special spot. It even has a light on the helmet so you can pretend to go caving in the dark! I knew I wanted to give this to you, but then I started thinking more about the whole wetsuit. You do look like a caver from Wookey Hole," Lady looked at me in my wetsuit and helmet. It seemed like she was taking her own brain picture.

I gave Lady a hug and many, many thank yous. I was so excited to play pretend adventures as a caver in Wookey Hole.

Lady was the perfect person to dream this with. She knew so much about Wookey Hole. We played inside the great room as we looked at her grandfather's adventurous pictures of Wookey Hole. Then, we played out in the garden as we dreamed even more about Wookey Hole.

Lady took my picture with her phone. I hoped that someday my picture could be up in the great room. Before I knew it, the sun was starting to set again. The light on my helmet came on and we both grinned.

Lady knew I didn't want to stop playing, so she got food for us and we ate in the backyard, I mean, on the floor of Wookey Hole!

I took my awesome helmet off and laid it carefully beside me. It was so special and so was my black and shiny wetsuit. I didn't have any more berries today. I tried the fried tomatoes with Wookey Hole Cheddar Cheese. It was so delicious. It tasted like cheesy goodness meets red deliciousness.

After I ate, I put my helmet back on, just like any caver would. Lady and I went to swing for a while after dinner. She hummed some ABC music. I enjoyed learning songs, as long as they were not opera songs. I think Lady knew this and was thinking about me. The ABC song sounds even better in my helmet!

I started thinking. Lady made me a wetsuit. She was totally thinking about me. Lady gave me the model of her grandfather's helmet. Lady played caving with me. Lady is totally my new best friend!

But what did I get for her? Nothing!

"Think, think, think," I repeated as I slowly turned away from Lady so I could figure out what to do. What would Lady like? I know she likes opera. She loves flowers. Lady told me all about Wookey Hole and the cheese. Then, the best idea came falling from the sky and landed straight in my brain! Some of my best ideas come falling from the sky and land in my brain.

"Let's go to the real Wookey Hole, Lady!"

"Bruno, it has been a long time since I have been there. Maybe holding onto my memories is better than starting something new all alone," Lady said sounding a little sad.

I gently smiled and replied, "But Lady, you wouldn't be alone, I'll go with you. You can show me all around the cave. Doesn't that sound like fun?"

Lady responded, "It would be fun to see Wookey Hole. I have missed the cave, but there is one problem, Bruno. Animals are not allowed to go inside the cave."

I said, "Wait, I heard that there are bats inside Wookey Hole. How come they get to be in there?"

As I was responding, I began to feel like I needed to open my backpack and use one of my tools.

Lady looked at her phone. She pulled up information about Wookey Hole.

"Sorry, Bruno. Bats live in the cave. It is their home. Unless you are a service dog, you are not allowed to go inside the real Wookey Hole. I won't go either, okay?" Lady said.

Lady seemed happy so I figured she wouldn't need to visit the real Wookey Hole because she was perfectly happy playing Wookey Hole at her home with me. But, deep down inside, I knew I was only thinking about what I wanted. I needed to remember that Lady thought about me when she made me my caving suit and helmet with the cool light. I carefully took my helmet off and started thinking of Lady. I took a breath in. I held it for the usual seven seconds, then I let the air and my negative feelings out. I stated with complete assurance, "Lady, you should go to Wookey Hole. You can tell me all about it when you get back."

Lady thought for a while. "It would be nice to see Wookey Hole again! I have missed it so much," she replied with her blue eyes sparkling in the moonlight. "I feel bad that I can't take you, Bruno, but it is the rule."

I knew what she was saying was true.

She picked up her phone and she told me that she bought her tour ticket to Wookey Hole online.

I nodded.

I wished that I could be a guide dog going to Wookey Hole, at least for a few hours. I could hold my head out the window and scream, "WEEEEEEEEEEE". I could wear a cool vest that said

"Service Dog. I'm on Duty." I thought that was so cool. Everyone would look up to me. Being a mouse, no one ever looks up to me.

I got ready to go to sleep. Lady made me new blue pajamas that she placed with care on my wonderful, new bed. I smiled my biggest smile and said, "Thank you for the presents, Lady. Thank you for being you and most of all, thank you for being my friend."

Lady smiled and gave me a big, good-night hug.

I looked at the moon as I dreamt about Wookey Hole. One lonely tear rolled down from my eye. I knew I was going to miss Lady, but it was important for her to see the place she liked so much.

I sat up in bed and took a deep breath in. I held it for seven seconds. When I let that deep breath out I also let the sadness wash away from my brain like the water in the River Axe. I wanted Lady to have fun, so I decided that I was going to be strong for her.

The next morning as I looked out the window, deep clouds of fog were all around. I could barely see the backyard. The sun was trying it's hardest to peek out through the thick fog. The fog felt gloomy, just like I did.

I decided to be happy for Lady. She was going to her favorite place that she missed so much! I had to be like the sun and shine through my cloud of sad thoughts.

Then, right after breakfast, Lady got ready for her trip. She got what she called "All dressed up." I didn't see it. I didn't know why she didn't wear a black, shiny wetsuit, like mine, to go to Wookey Hole.

Then Lady sat down beside me. I didn't know what

was going on. She calmly stated, "Okay, Bruno, you are going to be home alone for a while. "There are some rules to follow, okay?" Lady looked at me with a worried face. I nodded quickly.

"You can eat and play inside the house, but you can't go outside until I get back."

"It will be fun. You can use your imagination," Lady said as her face still looked worried.

"Do you have any questions?"

I nodded. I did have one question. I asked Lady, "What's imagination?"

Lady smiled her usual smile at me. "Bruno, imagination is dreaming about adventures anywhere or anytime. Does that sound like fun?"

I nodded again, but this time with a great big smile.

I explained as I carefully put my helmet on, "I am going to be a great explorer in Wookey Hole!"

Lady put on her hiking boots and her coat. She said, "The floor of Wookey Hole can get slippery. It's also usually cold inside."

I was beginning to feel better and better about using my imagination. At least I wasn't going to get cold or slip all around Wookey Hole while pretending inside of Lady's house!

I pulled my backpack onto my back. I adjusted the weights as I moved it from side to side. I was so thankful to have my tools and I was looking forward to my imagination taking me wherever it wanted to go.

Lady smiled. She seemed a little less nervous about things. She pulled out her own backpack. It didn't have straps for her back like mine. I guessed she would put tools inside. As I watched, Lady pressed buttons on her phone and then put it in her backpack. After that, she put something rectangular inside of her backpack. Lady told me that it's where she keeps her money. She also put dark glasses in her backpack. On that foggy day, she wasn't going to need them, but maybe Lady tries to shine through, just like me. After that Lady did something super strange. She put stuff on her face! I have no idea why she did that. Then, she put the stuff she put on her face inside her backpack with the weird straps. But, the last thing she put inside was the best thing she put in there! Lady put some Wookey Cheddar Cheese all wrapped up in paper inside her backpack! I do love cheese.

"Oh, no," Lady screamed! "Where are my keys?" She started running around the house looking everywhere. I didn't know what keys were but I thought that running around might be part of a game. I started running around, too. "Oh, there they are on the counter," Lady said in a relieved voice. As she reached for her keys, she dropped her backpack with the weird straps. I ran to help her pick it up, but before I knew what was happening, everything got all dark, except for the light on my helmet.

And then it happened. Lady closed her backpack with me in it! I could hear her yelling from inside the backpack, "Goodbye, Bruno! I hope you have a fun day!"

I screamed, "HELP, LADY! I'M INSIDE YOUR BACKPACK WITH WEIRD STRAPS! HELP!!!" But it was too late. Lady couldn't hear me!

SLAM! VROOM VROOM!

I asked the little air that was in Lady's backpack, "What's going on?" I screamed and screamed, "LADY, LADY, LADY!" And then it happened. More

opera! I sank back down into her backpack. I was
stuck in her backpack with the weird straps! I had
to think, think, think. I saw her phone and got an
idea. I followed the directions Lady gave me to turn
on my music. I was hoping to turn my music up to
get her attention and let her know that I was in her
backpack. When I followed the directions to turn on
the phone, all I saw was a picture of a speaker with
a line through it. No sound came out of the phone!

I needed to get out of her backpack! I opened my
backpack, pulled out the paper that I traced Lady's
hand on, and curled up into it to keep calm as I tried
to think of a way to get out. After I calmed down a
bit, I was able to think better. I focused my brain on
finding a solution and I was able to come up with a
plan!

I remembered when Lady took my picture when she
gave me my shiny, black wetsuit. Then, it came to
me! I was going to take pictures to let Lady know

I was in her backpack with the weird straps! There was a light that was stronger than my helmet light that kept flashing in my eyes! I took pictures of myself jumping up and down and yelling, "HELP," over, and over again until the bright light made my eyes all blurry.

I sat down in the backpack just to rest for a while. I tried everything, but nothing worked. I took my helmet off and put it right beside me. The light on my helmet was still glowing through the darkness. Then, I stretched out on the rectangular thingy. It was almost, but not quite as nice as my bed. I hoped to be able to hear about Wookey Hole through the backpack with weird straps. Before I knew it, I started to doze off and dream. I dreamed of the amazing Wookey Hole and I was actually going there for real! "Are we at Wookey Hole yet, Lady?" I said as I tried to sleep. Oh, how I wished Lady could hear me.

# Chapter 7

All night long, I tossed and turned. I was in a terrible dream where I was trapped inside a dark place! No matter how hard I tried, I couldn't figure a way out! When I woke up, I rubbed my eyes and looked around only to realize that it wasn't a dream! I was actually in Lady's backpack!

Everywhere I looked, it was dark. I picked up my backpack and swung it onto my back. After I put my goggles on, I was able to see the glow from the light on my helmet. I walked toward it, reached for my helmet, and held it in my hand. I looked all around.

What a mess! Lady's rectangular money holder was my one and only place to sleep and it was turned upside down! Coins were coming out of my bed! As I tried to turn my bed back over, it started attacking me! It was heavy! I pushed it off me and I fell straight down!

I pushed the bed off my legs and looked around the backpack. Lady's face stuff moved all around, too, and it made me sneeze! I sneezed so many times, I lost count! Her dark sunglasses were in her backpack. I still wondered why she would need sunglasses inside a cave. Then, I stood completely still realizing something. Lady's phone was missing!

All of a sudden, my feelings went into a downward spiral. I had no idea what to do with my time without Lady's phone! There was no music. There were no selfies. I started to tug at my backpack. I thought and thought for at least seven seconds when I thought a great thought!

I was sure that Lady had gotten her phone while I was sleeping. As soon as she looked at the pictures of me, I knew she would rescue me and I would be saved!

I took a moment to close my eyes. After that moment passed, I opened my eyes and walked around the backpack. I took a deep breath in and got ready to let it go when I recognized a wonderful smell! I raced to see if the smell was what I hoped it was. As I climbed closer and closer, the smell became stronger and stronger. I saw a yellowish-orange glow. It was the cheese that Lady put in her backpack! It looked beautiful! As I reached out to grab it, it fell through my hands! It was now buried at the bottom of her backpack! I put my helmet on and scurried down to the bottom of the darkness that surrounded me. I saw my light shining on the cheese! It was even more amazing to look at than before. It was so close, but Lady's stuff was holding it tight. I knew it was a good time to use one of my tools, so I opened my backpack and looked through it.

I came up with a great plan. I pulled out the yellow ribbon. I was going to try to throw it on top of the cheese. I took my helmet off and watched the light glaring at the cheese. The first time I tried, it didn't work. The second time I tried, it didn't work. It didn't even work the third time I tried! I wasn't going to give up now. I wanted that cheese!

I stood tall and whirled the yellow ribbon into the air! I made a large circle above my head before it fell to the ground. The yellow ribbon didn't catch the cheese! I took a deep breath in. I let it out slowly. I was determined to get that cheese! I took another breath in and let go of my negative thoughts.

I swung the yellow ribbon around my head as fast it would go. Try after try, the ribbon would fall to the ground. I was hungry and I wanted that cheese badly, so I would not give up! Just when my arms were getting too tired to go on, the yellow ribbon circled the cheese! I pulled and pulled through all of Lady's things to get the cheese. After reaching out for it and not giving up, I had my prize! I held it tightly in my hands and stared at its' yellow glow. I smiled as I took a big whiff of its delicious smell. I wanted to enjoy every bite of this cheese. I slowly brought the cheese up to my mouth and gave it a big kiss! After thinking about it for three seconds, I took one big bite out of the amazing cheese and then put the rest back into my backpack for later.

I was so happy Lady had brought Wookey Hole Cheddar Cheese for emergencies because this was definitely an emergency! Of course, you need air and water in an emergency, but cheese is the most important. I was sure of it, even if I don't know everything, I was sure of this one!

After eating, I pushed my body against the wall of

the backpack. I looked at my helmet sitting beside me. All she would have to do was look back at her pictures. How long would that take? I had no idea, but I believed it wouldn't be too long.

As I kept looking at my light, it made me think of the sun. I missed the sun shining on me. The sun was there when I started my walk through the meadow. The sun was there when I met everybody. It was there in the morning to wake me up and say hello. This day was different. I was in the backpack and it was so dark and lonely. I had a bad dream that came true! I needed to have the sun glowing on me. I wanted to see the sun. I knew I would feel better with the warmth of the sun on my face. As I thought about the sun, I knew it was staring back at me wondering how I ever got stuck in Lady's backpack. I couldn't see the sun, but I knew it was always there.

I began to dream of the sun looking down on me

in Lady's beautiful garden. I heard birds singing and saw the roses swaying in the wind. I saw Lady planting and when I focused hard enough, I could even smell the flowers! As I was thinking, I heard 'drip, drip, drip' sounds. In England, it rains a lot. I laid down and closed my eyes. With a stomach full of cheese, the sound of the rain, and the dreams of Lady's garden, I began to fall back to sleep. I was minding my own business when all of a sudden, the walls of Lady's backpack were moving! All of Lady's stuff started falling on top of me!

SLAM! SLAM!

I started to flip in the air! Everything was moving up! I tightened the grip of my backpack and put my helmet on. I needed my tools more than ever! I held onto everything tightly. I thought maybe Lady and I had arrived at Wookey Hole, but I didn't know for sure until I heard her kind voice.

"Hi there! I bought my tour ticket on the Wookey Hole website. I printed it out for you. Hold on, I have it here somewhere." Lady was talking to someone, but I didn't know who. As she opened her backpack, I yelled, "I'm right inside your backpack. Get me out of here, PLEEEEEASE!"

I climbed faster than I had ever climbed in my entire life! I had to get all the way to the top so she could see me!

"Wait, I forgot, I have it in my coat pocket," Lady thought out loud.

And just like that, Lady closed the backpack with the weird straps. My heart sank as I moved back down into the backpack. I had to find something to do. I was so disappointed. I felt sadness bubbling up to the surface of my body.

Then I heard a deep voice speaking to Lady. "Thank

you for your ticket. Here is a sticker for the day. You can go through Wookey Hole as many times as you would like before the end of the day. You can also check out the other sites around the cave. Enjoy your tour."

The voice paused for three seconds then it started again proudly saying, "I'm a caver here at Wookey Hole. My name is Bill."

I felt relieved to have Bill and Lady in my life because that meant that I have two friends to help me out of Lady's backpack.

Lady began to speak but I didn't hear what she said. I was too busy thinking about how to get Lady and Bill's attention. No matter how much I yelled, no one heard me say a word. I started to feel lonely. Before I could feel really sorry for myself, it all started again.

The backpack began to move again. Things continued to fall but this time I played a new game of dodge the objects. And just when I began to have fun and get good at the game, everything stopped moving! With my ear on the wall, I heard the drip, drip, drip sound of the rain. I started tapping my foot to the beat of the rain. I breathed in and let the air out slowly. I started making up sounds. My head started moving back and forth slowly. I was getting a slow, sad beat in my head that matched my mood. Then I heard a small sound so I stopped humming. I pressed my whole face against the backpack wall so both of my ears could hear. I overheard amazing sounds! I could hear the best laughing sounds, but it didn't sound like Lady's laughter. It didn't sound like the cavers either. It sounded like children! I remembered seeing them in the meadow with their parents, a long, long time ago.

Thinking back, I remembered children running and laughing in the meadow as they raced around and

watched the butterflies flying by. They pretended
they were flying like the winged creatures and the
dandelions fluttering in the air. The children were
laughing with each other as everyone waited for the
tour to begin. I pushed my head even further against
the side of the backpack with all my strength. I
wanted to know what they were playing! How I
wished I could see through the backpack!

I slumped back down against the wall and I began
to think again. I missed Lady and I wondered if she
was missing me the way I missed her.

I heard the drip, drip, drip sound of more rain. I was
sure that the sun was worried about me. I wasn't in
the mood to hum anymore. I just listened.

I waited and waited for at least seven seconds. I
took a breath in and let it out. The voices kept on
talking as we started moving all over again. I could
feel each step Lady took. Even though I was trapped

inside Lady's backpack, it still made me feel good that I was with her.

I heard many things, but what I liked most was when a deep voice said, "Kids, hold onto my hands when we get inside the cave." I knew it was a parent who cared about his kids. I wanted Lady to care about me that way.

I pulled out my rolled-up paper that held Lady's traced hand. I was so glad I made this in the kitchen with her. I zipped up my backpack and held onto my paper hand. I was so ready for Wookey Hole. Even though I was the only one listening to me, I still said, "I want to learn all about Wookey Hole."

In a loud, clear voice, I heard Bill say, "Welcome to Wookey Hole. My name is Bill and I will be your tour guide today."

As he continued to talk, Lady and the tour group

kept on moving. I knew everyone was moving because everything in her backpack was getting jumbled again.

"This is the Wookey Witch," said Bill.

I remembered Lady talking about it. Feeling bold, I stared at the backpack wall and said, "You don't scare me!"

I knew it was just a rock, but to be safe, I crawled all the way to the bottom of Lady's backpack and curled up like the hedgehog.

Lady's backpack began moving again. I could see lights and hear music going off and on. I wanted to hear better. I pushed my ear to the side of the backpack so I would be able to learn about Wookey Hole. I thought about what Lady told me about my imagination. I wanted to try to use my brain pictures so I could not only hear about the cave but also picture it. I moved to the edge again. I closed my eyes so I could imagine Wookey Hole.

Bill continued on with his speech, "Wookey Hole is one of the largest cave systems in all of England, even if a lot of it is underwater. It is a limestone and weathering cave. The River Axe runs all the way through the cave. With all the rain and underground water, over the years, Wookey Hole's rock formations change. There is a large rock that looks like a dinosaur. There is a cave wall full of shapes that look like lace as the water drips down through Wookey Hole. There are also rock formations that swirl around into perfect circles.

Bill described the rocks. He told the tour group, Lady, and I all about different rocks and how they were formed. He explained that there were two main types of rocks in the cave: stalagmites and stalactites.

"Take my picture by the big rock, pleeease, Daddy," said a child's on the tour. I hoped Lady was taking pictures with her phone so I could see them later. I wanted to hear more from Bill. He knew a lot about Wookey Hole. I crawled up to the top of the backpack.

Bill kept on with his talk about rocks in Wookey Hole. "Stalactites are rocks that form at the ceiling of the cave and work their way down. Some are tall rocks and some are short rocks."

As the tour group walked on with Bill, I could tell when Lady moved. I was moving right with her in her backpack. I didn't mind the movement. This was a great adventure. I wondered what was next on the tour.

"The next portion of the cave has a drop that is approximately 110 feet straight down into darkness."

Bill continued with a monotone voice, "This is your opportunity to show off your caving skills as you hold on to the walls of the cave. But whatever you do, don't look down."

I knew Bill's voice was different after talking about the darkness. It reminded me of the time he was reading to the trees in the meadow when I first met him. It sounded like his voice was programmed with what to say. Those weren't Bill's words.

I could hear all the sounds from the tour group. Parents of the children who had been laughing before, now yelled at them, "Don't let go of my hand!"

I could tell that Bill waited as parents held tightly to their children's hands. In Bill's usual voice, he stated, "There is no need to panic. There is a perfectly good bridge to walk across for this part." I heard the group laugh as they walked past Bill thinking he was trying to be funny. As Lady moved, I could hear the tour group oo-ing and ah-ing over the straight drop into darkness. I climbed deep into the backpack and held on. I was experienced at falling, but I didn't want to fall into complete darkness!

"Everyone, I would like you all to look at our cheese room. This is the room where we keep our world-famous cheddar cheese. It is kept here since the cave is as cold as a refrigerator. Wookey Hole Cheese is stored and aged here and has a taste like no other," Bill said.

I was jumping up and down! I could hear people taking pictures.

"Lady, please take lots of pictures of this," I yelled jumping up and down. It must be amazing. I could even smell the cheese. It smelled sooooooo gooooooood!

I pressed my entire body close to the backpack wall. I reached out with my hand. I so wanted to touch it!

Lady started moving away from the cheese! I yelled, "No, wait! Lady, go back! Don't go!!!"

It was too late. Lady was moving away from the cheese. I waved good-bye to the famous Wookey Hole cheddar cheese room. So near, yet so far!

Bill talked to the tour group as he walked along. "There are three cave systems that can connect to Wookey Hole. They are close by, but no one has been able to create a route that we can build to join them all together. The water is high and the spaces are narrow in the caves. Many cavers throughout the years have attempted to find a way through. My maps and studies show that this dark pool of water right here leads out of this cave and would be the best way to connect the other caves," Bill shared.

I thought of Lady's grandfather. He was a caver at Wookey Hole. Lady told me that he was one of the many that tried to find a route to connect the caves. Then, I thought about Lady. I knew she was thinking about her grandfather, too.

"Thank you for visiting today. I hope you enjoyed the wonders of Wookey Hole. If you have any questions, please ask me. If you wish to proceed this way, you will come to more attractions at Wookey Hole. Stop at our gift shop on the way out for a souvenir from your tour. You can also purchase Wookey Hole cheddar cheese there."

I heard people clapping. I started clapping, too. Bill did a good job teaching us about the cave. That is when it happened.

The backpack started to tip over, all I could think about was climbing to the top of the backpack as quickly as I could, just like before, but faster! The backpack was tipping, and I knew it would soon hit the rocks and that would be painful, just like my not so terrific flip and the thorn in the garden!

I needed to hurry! It was good that Lady's stuff started falling inside of her backpack. I used her falling items to jump from one thing to another. I was moving fast but at the same time, I was able to feel my body move in slow motion. I didn't want to get smushed under all her stuff!

The backpack landed on the ground of the cave and it opened up, causing all of Lady's stuff to go in different directions!

My eyes slowly adjusted as I moved my goggles into place. Lady was picking stuff up, using the flashlight on her phone to see. I took my helmet off and put it carefully in my backpack. I got up to follow Lady, but before I knew it, she was gone! I looked to the left. No one. I looked to the right. Still no one. I

couldn't find her anywhere! I shouted, "LADY!!! LADY!!! LADY!!!" But then the strangest thing happened. I heard my words come back to me, not one or two times, but three times!

Lady must not have heard me. I sat back down to think. Maybe, I should stay right here and wait for Lady to come back for me. I waited and waited for at least seven seconds. I knew because I took my usual breath in and out to let my brain do its best thinking.

Lady didn't come back for me. It was dark in Wookey Hole. I had enough of darkness in Lady's backpack.

I thought back to what Bill had said about the tour. I also thought about Lady and how well she knows me. I was sure that Lady would know that I didn't want to meet the Wookey Witch. I was not going in that direction for sure. Then, there was the straight drop into darkness. I wasn't going near that on my own! Bill told us a lot about rocks. I looked around. Rocks were everywhere! I thought and thought, but I couldn't remember the word Bill used.

## Chapter 8

"Sta-lag-a-kites... That wasn't it. Sta-lag-a-nights... That wasn't it either." Then I remembered. "Sta-lag-MICE!!"

Suddenly, I got an idea that fell from the sky and straight through the cave ceiling of Wookey Hole!

I excitedly said out loud, "I could go to the Famous Wookey Hole cheddar cheese room!"

Lady was going to see pictures of me, I just knew she would. She would probably be thinking about me inside Wookey Hole and would race to the cheese room because she would know that's where I would go. I was sure of it!

I unzipped my backpack and held my helmet in my hand. If I was going to find my way to Lady and the cheese room, I had to get started.

I knew my nose would take me in the right direction. I could smell the cheese! I love Wookey Hole Cheddar Cheese! I was determined to find Lady! With my circle pointer and my nose, I was going to find that room. Feeling confident, I put my helmet on and started walking along, all by myself.

While I was walking, I felt eyes staring at me. The eyes followed me as I walked. I stopped. The eyes stopped. I started to walk faster. The eyes were still following me but faster now. In fact, the eyes were attached to wings! I suspected that it was one of the bats of Wookey Hole.

I stopped and I took my helmet off again. I could smell food. It smelled different, but oh so good. I walked so far, and I didn't know if I could go on! My belly was making rumbling sounds! I had to have that food!

I dragged my left foot and then my right. I saw the eyes continuing to look at me. I wanted the bat to understand what a hard time I was having, so I brought all my drama out with my words.

I said in agony, "I can't go another step without food! If only there was someone here to share some food with me! I'm so hungry I could eat a whole cow!"

Slowly floating down from above, like a feather to the ground, the bat came closer. With a worried look, the bat said, "Are you okay?"

"I've been walking forever in this darkness! I feel like I will faint if I don't eat soon. I don't suppose you have any food, do you? Well, do you have any food?" I asked, feeling impatient. I couldn't get my stomach to stop rumbling!

"I'm Ava. I live here at Wookey," the bat said using her best manners.

"Hi, Ava. My name is Bruno, I've heard about you from Bill," I said still very hungry.

Looking a bit confused at my answer, Ava said, "How do you know my Bill?"

Rubbing my belly, I said, "I'll tell you about it after we eat, ok?"

Ava nodded yes and we sat down on the cave floor.

Ava pulled some more of her food out from her collection of tools. She had a spreader, graham squares, creamy marshmallows in a can, and dark, delicious, melted, sweet squares. Ava put it all together and handed it to me. The food was so good. I called it sticky, sweet treat, but Ava told me the snack was called some more squares.

We ate and ate until my tummy was full.

I liked the some more snack, but there was one problem. This great snack needed a better name. I didn't know what, but some more squares just wasn't it. I hoped that one day, someone could come up with a better name.

After we ate, we cleaned up the floor of the cave by eating all the crumbs. I was telling Ava how I cleaned up the meadow after watching people. That is how I found cheese and other things. I told Ava all about the day I found the circle pointer. She looked up at it with wonder in her glowing eyes.

I got a good look at Ava. She looked sort of like a caver herself. She wore a brown explorer hat with a strap so it wouldn't fall off when she was flying. She had dark curly hair with dark eyes that glowed like my cool light. The best detail about Ava's outfit was what she wore around her waist! She had a belt that looked a lot like Bill's tools. She had tools, too!

"Okay, Bruno, how do you know my Bill," Ava said again. She just had to know.

"I meet Bill with the other cavers as they walk to Wookey Hole. I have never been to Wookey Hole before, I told her. I had a question for Ava too, so I said, "Why do you call him my Bill?"

"I call him my Bill because we have been friends for a long time. I'm sorta in charge when he explores the cave. I fly over him. I tell him which way to go. Yeah, I'm in charge...of getting lost! I get lost a lot! Okay, I get lost all the time! Bill shares his cheese and bread lunches with me. I eat the bread and save the cheese. I used to try to leave trails of cheese, but the other bats would always eat them. Wait, have you seen my Bill?" Ava wanted to know where he could be.

I was too busy thinking about my own thoughts. I said, "I would love to call Lady, my Lady. I think she would really like that. It sounds so English!" I wondered to myself if there are any other 'my Ladys' as kind as her in England.

"Wait, this is your first time visiting Wookey Hole and you are walking around like you know where everything is. How do you do that?" Ava asked.

Before I could say a word, Ava continued to talk, "I have lived here all of my life and I still get lost every single day! Can you teach me how to get around like you do? I'm tired of always getting lost and the other bats teasing me!"

"Well, I follow my nose and my circle pointer. They will lead me in the right direction. They haven't ever failed me," I said with pride. Up until that point, no one had ever asked me for help before.

"I don't have a circle pointer but I do have a nose. Help me use it like you do, please," Ava begged.

"Well, I first put my nose to the ground and follow the scent," I tried to give clear directions. "Do you smell cheese?"

Ava listened to me and now had her nose on the floor of the cave. She shook her head no and shrugged her bat shoulders.

"I smell cheese coming from that direction. My circle pointer agrees with my nose. We should go there, I said boldly.

"Lady has been so kind to me. We both like to dance and talk and eat. We both needed company. She makes me laugh. I make her laugh. We like the same things and sometimes we like different things, but we are friends," and with that, I told Ava all about my Lady (I really like saying that).

Before long, I had reached the Wookey Hole cheddar cheese room! It was beautiful!!!

There were Wookey Hole cheese circles that looked right at me! There was cheese that went on forever! I stared at it for some time. The circle cheese stared back at me. It was a beautiful sight! Keeping my helmet on, I went running into the famous Wookey Hole cheddar cheese room for a closer look. As I went faster and faster, my feet started slipping on the wet cave floor. I was water skiing and having a blast when...

POW!!!

I fell flat. As I opened my eyes, I saw a super cool guy looking right at me! I waved. He waved at the same time I did. I danced. He danced at the same time I did. I tried to trick him by leaning to the left side and then pushing my body as quickly as I could go to the right side. He did just what I did, at the same time as me! He was so crafty!

I stared at him and he stared at me. I wanted to know who this guy was.

I thought and thought. This was familiar. I took a

three second brain break. I took off my helmet and fixed my goggles that were falling down my face. I wanted to look good for Lady, so I fixed my hair. The super cool guy fixed his hair at the same time!

I wanted to figure this out so I reached out to touch him on the shoulder, but it was a shiny, hard surface, instead. It was me the whole time!

This was like the puddles in the meadow, only hard. This hard stuff was way better since it had cheese in it! I turned around and smiled at all the real cheese looking right at me. I stared at it for three long breaths in and out.

I kept looking at Wookey Hole cheese and my smile got bigger and bigger. I started jumping up and down and clapping because I was so excited to be in the best place of all of Wookey Hole.

I looked around again to see if Lady was there but

she wasn't in the cheese room.

And then I stopped. Clapping and jumping reminded me of Lady. I missed Lady, I mean my Lady, so much!

I slumped down on the cave floor.

Out of breath from flying, Ava arrived and said in a big deep breath, "Bruno, what's wrong? Don't you like cheese? You are a mouse. Why are you so sad?"

I told her about the day I first met Lady and how nice she was. I needed to find her. I was hoping that she had seen the pictures and come to my favorite place in Wookey Hole. I could only point to the circle cheese. I couldn't talk anymore.

Tears were pushing their way out of my eyes. I tried to stop them, but they broke through and rolled down my face like a waterfall. I was able to keep the tears back through everything else that had happened!

I was trapped inside Lady's backpack. I explored Wookey Hole, in a way. I survived a rocky fall from the backpack! I found my way to the cheese room, my favorite place, but my Lady wasn't there.

I stopped to think and reset my brain. I pulled my thinking stone out of my backpack. Ava flew down and asked me about it.

"What is that," Ava questioned in a soft voice looking at how I was feeling.

"It is my thinking stone. When I don't know what to do, I hold it in my hand and try to reset my brain. Then, I focus and work on solving my problems," I said in between sniffles. I wondered if it still worked, so I shook it in my hand as I tried to stop crying. I told Ava about my tools and that I carry them with me for help.

Ava nodded. She flew high up to the roof of the cave and then in a circle around me. She didn't say a word. She gave me time to calm my body and my brain.

After taking my seven-second breath in and releasing all my feelings into the cave air, I looked up at Ava. She wasn't flying anymore. She stopped flying around and was sitting on a rock with her glowing eyes moving back and forth.

Ava started to get an idea. It was a little idea at first and then her eyes started glowing even brighter. Her idea came bursting forth, "Where did Lady drop the backpack? When I lose something, I always go back to where I lost it. Maybe she is waiting there!"

I told Ava how wise I thought she was. I could tell

that made her feel good. She had a great big smile on her face. We both raced back to the end of the tour. That was where the backpack opened. I ran quickly. Ava followed me as she flew from high above.

I got to the end of the tour. Sadly, there was no Lady. Her backpack wasn't there either.

Ava finally arrived after her long flight through the cave. She was out of breath again. As she flew to a rock to sit and cool down, she asked me, "Bruno, where's your Lady?"

I shrugged my shoulders and sadly said, "She isn't here either, Ava!"

Ava stared at me with her dark glowing eyes. She didn't know what to say. She said nothing at all.

I pulled on the straps of my backpack. I took a deep

breath and then I let it out. I put my helmet back on and opened my backpack, but this time I took my weighted blanket out. I didn't know what to do. Hungry and scared, I ate all of the cheese that Lady had put in my backpack. One single tear rolled down my face. I felt all alone, even though I had Ava. I put my weighted blanket over my head as I sat on the cave floor.

I started feeling sorry for myself. I was scared and it was dark. I wanted my Lady to come back for me. I wanted Bill to come and find me. But Bill and my Lady weren't there. I cried a little bit more.

Ava flew around my head and started whistling a song. It was so soothing. It helped me calm down. I was glad I wasn't really alone. It was good to have Ava to talk to and help me with my problems. After I calmed down a bit, I put the blanket back into my backpack.

Ava saw that I was doing better so she came down to talk with me some more. She told me all about her adventures with Bill. Proudly she said, "My Bill keeps a notebook, has maps, and works really hard to find a way that will connect all the caves. The other cavers don't think he can do it. They eat their food like Jerk Chicken, Indian Butter Chicken, and Welsh Rarebit while they laugh at my Bill! The other cavers say things like, "Give up, Bill," but that just makes him work harder. My Bill is the most brilliant person I know." She paused for less than three seconds and kept on talking. "Did you know that Wookey Hole is one of the largest cave systems in all of England, even if a lot of it is underwater," Ava said, quoting Bill's facts.

Ava continued to talk about her Bill. "Sometimes he works so hard that his eyes move so fast with ideas and his body rocks back and forth. That was my cue to calm Bill down by saying his important words, "You can do this. Don't give up. Keep on trying."

After that Bill takes a deep breath in and calms down.

"Since most of Wookey Hole is underwater, Bill and the cavers go diving a lot," Ava stated.

"Yes, he should be here anytime. I don't know what could be keeping him. Unless he already went in the water when we were in the cheese room," Ava said calmly as she thought out loud.

"He and the cavers could be in the water. He goes through that dark pool of water over there. All his maps lead to that being the way out of Wookey Hole," Ava said proudly about her Bill. "It is also the way to connect to the other caves."

"I am determined to find my Lady. This water doesn't look that deep," I said looking down into it as my heart beat faster and faster.

"Don't go, Bruno. You can stay here! Bill can visit us. Wookey Hole is a nice place to live, please stay Bruno. Pleeeeeeease!" Ava begged.

I shook my head no. Ava looked at me with serious eyes. "I like your caving gear but, have you ever gone caving for real?" Ava asked with a worried look on her face.

I shook my head no and looked down at the cave floor.

"Bruno, it is my duty as a caver to teach you how to safely go underwater caving," Ava spoke in a teacher's voice.

I looked at Ava with a question mark on my face. How would she be able to help me?

"Bruno, I may not have gone in the water, but I do hear all the directions. I can repeat it all back to you. I may get lost a lot, but I remember everything I have heard," Ava continued with that voice.

"Are you ready to get started now?" Teacher Ava asked.

I nodded yes.

"You need to understand how to breathe underwater. You don't have gills like a fish, so you will be using S.C.U.B.A." Ava took a short breath and continued to talk more. "That stands for Self Contained Underwater Breathing Apparatus. Bill has extra small oxygen tanks that I can connect to your suit. I will then seal your helmet closed so that water does not get inside. Underwater cavers use hand signals to talk," Teacher Ava was on a roll. She explained all the hand signals.

I was too nervous to say that I didn't understand what she was talking about. I just nodded my head and she kept going over all the technical stuff. She said to use hand signals. I wonder if this was what the swan was trying to use that day in the meadow, so long ago.

"After that, I will need rope to tie around your waist so that you will have a way back if you can't make it out. If Bill and the other cavers are already in the water, follow their guideline. The guideline is a rope that has been secured and has clips on it. You need to grab onto the clips through the water if it's there," Ava said.

"I have the extra oxygen that I can put on your suit. I have the what we need to close your helmet tight. I just need rope," Ava looked around as she spoke.

I pulled the yellow ribbon out of my backpack. I remembered the day Lady gave me the present tied with the yellow ribbon. Not only was I wearing her present, but I was going to be using the yellow ribbon. I held the yellow ribbon high up in the air for Ava. She smiled and reached for the yellow ribbon.

As Ava worked to get everything ready, I thought even further back. I have come so far, been so many places, met new people, but all I could think about was my Lady.

I stopped daydreaming and heard Ava say, "This is perfect. I will tie it around your waist and then wrap it around that rock over there. Then I will connect your oxygen and close your helmet. We will use hand signals to talk. Do you have any other questions about underwater caving?" Ava asked since she wanted to make sure she covered all the directions she learned from the cavers.

I shook my head no. I couldn't believe I was really going to do this. I had to find my Lady! We worked together to get it all ready. Ava had water stay-away spray for my backpack. She made sure everything stayed dry in my backpack. Ava got extra oxygen from her tools that fit my wetsuit perfectly. The oxygen was connected to my suit. I thought, "This is really going to happen!"

Ava got a tube of super-strong underwater glue from her tools. She put it all around the outside of my helmet. It was closed tight so that there was no way water would get inside. Ava tapped on my helmet when the glue was dry. With the helmet on tight, I wasn't going to be able to hear Ava. It was a good thing we sorta practiced those hand signals!

The yellow ribbon was tied around me and then Ava flew with her end of the yellow ribbon and wrapped it many times around the nearest rock.

Before she counted down, just as Bill and the cavers did each day, Ava flew near my ear and said as loud as she could, "YOU CAN DO THIS! DON'T

GIVE UP! KEEP ON TRYING!"

I took a deep breath. I held it in for extra-long this time, then I let go of the negative, scary feelings I had. I was floating in the dark pool and waiting for Ava's countdown.

With my eyes just above the water, I stared at Ava so I could follow all her directions.

I could barely hear her yell with the water all around me and my helmet sealed tight, "Three more go!" Or maybe she said, "Thumbs go low!" I didn't know what Ava said. I stared at her not knowing if there were three divers or do I let my thumbs dive first. I wasn't sure what she said so I just floated in the water. Maybe, I should have listened closer to Ava's diving instructions.

As I floated, I saw her. I couldn't believe it! I looked over to see my Lady running and jumping up! She was waving at me! She was mouthing something, but I couldn't hear her. I just stared at her with squinting eyes, saying loudly, "WHAT DID YOU SAY?" Even though I couldn't hear her, I wanted to get out of the water to talk to her. I looked over at Ava who was talking to Bill, as he came running in. Ava told him about everything that was going on.

Lady screamed, "I've been looking for you everywhere, Bruno! I saw the pictures on my phone! I'm so sorry you got stuck inside my purse!" With worry in her voice, she yelled, "Bruno, I LOVE YOU!!!"

I pushed and pulled against the water. Our hands touched for one long second, but it was too late! With tears in her eyes, Lady yelled once again, "DON'T GO!!!"

The current of the River Axe was too strong for me! It was pulled me down as I fought against the

current to stay with my friend, my Lady. The last thing I saw before being pulled underwater was Bill and Ava trying to grab the yellow ribbon that had fallen off the rock! It was being pulled down into the water, just like me!

I tried to climb up the yellow ribbon to my Lady, but it didn't work. I couldn't move! The current of the River Axe had me and it wasn't going to let go!

As I tumbled through River Axe, my head started spinning. I worked harder and harder to pull myself up and start swimming through the water. I was hitting rock after rock as I went by. I kept on going with the flow of River Axe. To be the first discoverer of this new cave, I needed to stop and explore but the pull of the water was too strong. It was taking me on another journey!

## Chapter 9

This wild ride reminded me of my long journey through the meadow, only a lot rockier! Back then, I didn't know who I would find. I met others along the way. I met swan who wouldn't talk to me and I don't know why. I scared a hedgehog, even though I didn't mean to. A puffy white sheep had a good laugh along the way because of me, and I met some cavers. The best caver I knew was Bill. He saw me and even talked with me. Bill is brilliant. I so needed his help through all of this!

I like that my Lady listens to me. She cares about me. We have fun together. She helps me. She cares for her plants and me with the biggest heart. Lady started to teach me how to read and write. We had so much fun talking and laughing in her thatched roof house. She even let me stay in her home.

When I was trying to help her, I got stuck in her backpack with the weird straps and went on a long trip to Wookey Hole. At first, I didn't see much of the cave, but I did get to hear about it from inside Lady's backpack with Bill as our tour guide.

I fell out of the backpack and met my new friend, Ava. Ava shared food with me. She was good company when I was looking for the famous cheddar cheese room of Wookey Hole. When I was super sad, she was there with me and made sure I was safe in the deep, dark pool of water when I tried to look for Lady. Ava didn't know that Lady would find me and that I didn't need to get in the water.

I had to make the best of it. I had plenty of oxygen because Ava made sure of that. I had the helmet light that Lady gave me. I was on the path that was connected to the other caves and would lead me out of Wookey Hole. Bill told Ava that this would work. I looked down at my circle pointer. It confirmed that I was going the right way. River Axe had been a great help getting me here. All I had to do was trust my friends and not give up so I kept on swimming and swimming.

I tried to think about how Bill led the tour around Wookey Hole. If I was giving a tour in the deep, dark water, I would talk about all the rocks, just like Bill did. As I swam, my brain started having fun as I imagined the circular rock to be a sheep! I saw a long-eared rock with a puffy tail that looked like a rabbit! I even saw a long-necked rock that looked like a graceful swan!

Inside the cave were narrow paths to slide through.

A slide is fun wherever you go, but it made it extra fun to slip up and down as I swam! "WEEEEE!"

I saw a fish that swam by and stared at me. I noticed salmon, trout, and kingfish. I bowed as the kingfish swam by me, but there was one problem. The kingfish was missing his crown! It must have fallen off when he was swimming through these narrow paths. I knew he would need it back, so I kept my eyes open wide so that I would see it if it floated by. Poor Kingfish!

As I was looking down for the crown, a rock ran into my head! POW!!! My head began to ache and I started to feel dizzy. My arms and legs were getting tired. I had to find a place to rest for a while. I kept on swimming until I saw the most unbelievable sight!

I saw a large underground opening in the cave! The walls were super tall and there were large rocks to sit on to watch the River Axe flow by. I swam closer and closer with my eyes staring at it. I didn't want to miss this spot! The River Axe was pushing against me. The current was so much stronger than me! It didn't want me to have a chance to rest. With all my power, I pushed against the water and made it to the underground landing!

I was dripping wet from swimming, but my wetsuit kept the cold water away from me!

As I climbed onto the opening to rest, I sat down and I looked around.

It was amazing! I looked straight up at the tall cave wall that had water dripping down from it. As I moved my eye gaze up, my mouth dropped open and fell to the bottom of the underground watery cave floor! As I stared at the ceiling, all that would come out of my mouth was, "WOW!"

I looked at the squiggly lines on the cave walls

behind me as the water came down through this underground portion of Wookey Hole. It was amazing! I knew the water was strong, but I didn't know that it was such a great artist! As I closed my mouth, I remembered the places Ava told me to push against to open my helmet. I knew my body and brain needed a break so I carefully took off my helmet and placed it beside me so it would light up the wall.

I turned off the valve for oxygen that was attached to my suit. It was a good thing Ava knew all about underwater caving. She made sure I was safe. I looked down at my waist for the first time since being in the water. I saw the yellow ribbon still tied around my waist and gently tugged at it. It was still holding on to something above the dark pool that I came through. I felt a warm glow come over me. For the first time since being in the water, I didn't feel so lonely. It felt as if someone up above was holding onto my yellow ribbon.

I took a deep breath and held it for seven seconds.
As I let it out, I looked at River Axe flowing by. I
turned around, stared at the cave wall, and followed
the lines down. My head moved side to side with
the curves of the lines. It wasn't good for me to mix
back and forth movements with the headache I was
beginning to feel. My head started pounding more,
saying to me, "You're getting sleepy, oh so sleepy."
I fought to stay awake, but it was no use. I was
exhausted and needed to take a little cat nap.

As I slept, I kept moving through the water. My head
was pounding and I was lost! I felt like I was never
going to get out of there!

Then I woke up. I looked around and realized that
my bad dream was real! I was lost! I didn't know
which way to go. I curled my legs under my body
and started to feel like the hedgehog. My body
rocked back and forth. I felt like I would never see
my Lady again! That made me very sad because I

wanted to call her my Lady and I thought I would never get a chance to!

As I rocked harder and harder, I started to hold my breath in. There were a lot of negative feelings. For the first time, I didn't think I was going to get rid of them!

I yelled, "HOW WILL ANYONE FIND ME?" I leaned toward my sealed-up backpack when I heard my own voice over, and over again. Then it repeated softer and softer. I sat up. Why was my voice talking to me? I tried it out again, "HIIII, Hiii, hi." It was me again! I heard my voice over and over. It would start out strong, repeat, and then get softer and softer.

Then, I remembered the time when I called for Lady when I fell out of her backpack and she didn't hear me. I heard my own voice over, and over again that time, too. This must be like that.

As I stared at the huge cave ceiling, I longed to hear anyone else but myself but it was so silent. All I heard was the River Axe dripping away at the rocks! I kept on staring at the ceiling. There must be someone else to talk to besides me!

After about seven seconds, I heard talking. I listened closely. I could hear voices that I had heard before! I heard a kind voice. I heard a voice that had a lot to say, and I heard a supportive voice. My voices of hope! If you keep on trying and don't give up, there's hope out there! My hope was in voices! I thought more about the voices I heard. It was Lady, Bill, and Ava! They were my voices of hope! I knew they would try to help me! They were going to be my way out of there!

I could hear my Lady sobbing as she said, "Where is my Bruno? How will he know how to get out of here? I need to find him, now!"

Ava yelled, "Don't yell at my Bill! He needs time to think!" Ava went on to say, "Do you see what your words have made my Bill do? He is curled up into a ball and rocking. He cares a lot about Bruno. He also wants to help him. Do you think he can do his best thinking like this?"

I never heard Ava talk like this before. She was defending her Bill because she cared a lot about him.

Over and over again, Bill was saying, "I must help Bruno, I MUST HELP BRUNO, I MUST HELP BRUNO!" Each time Bill said this, he was sounding more and more upset. Bill wasn't upset with me. It sounded like Bill was upset with himself and he didn't know what to do except to use the same words over and over. This wasn't the sound of a voice of hope.

I heard Ava whistling as she had with me in Wookey

Hole when I was sad. I knew this was for her Bill.
Then I heard Ava say, "YOU CAN DO THIS! DON'T
GIVE UP! KEEP ON TRYING!"

"I'm so sorry for making you feel upset, Bill. I'm just
very worried about my Bruno. Please forgive me for
yelling," said Lady.

And then I heard Bill say, "I understand. Now, let
me think."

There were no more voices. I felt very lonely. I knew
Bill was doing his best thinking with it this quiet and
with Bill thinking, I knew I had my best chance of
getting out of this deep dark underground cave.

# Chapter 10

While I was waiting, I stared back at the amazing squiggly-lined, cave wall behind me. I followed each line down from the ceiling to the cave floor. My headache was gone. The moving of my eyes passed the time as Bill was thinking his best thoughts for me.

With a loud echo, I heard, "I know the directions Bruno should take," Bill said proudly. As he kept talking, I listened very carefully to each word he said.

"When Bruno went through the deep dark pond, River Axe's current was pulling him this way, so he must have kept on following it. I hope he found the underground landing with the huge squiggly-lined cave wall."

I looked behind myself. I found it. I kept on listening to find out more directions.

"After the squiggly-lined cave wall, Bruno needs to keep swimming," Bill said as he took a breath to think about what came next. He had so many directions in his head!

I took a deep breath in with all my insecure feelings and let it out as I remembered what Ava told me, "You've got this!" I had to follow all of Bill's directions.

Bill kept on going, "Next, Bruno will get to a low tunnel. It's good that he is a mouse. He wouldn't fit otherwise. This is the place we have gotten stuck before." Bill stopped for a while.

With my ears perked up at the cave ceiling, I could hear Bill talking again.

"After the tunnel, Bruno will come to a spiky-rock formation that looks like a hedgehog. When he has passed that rock, he will see a rock that he has to climb over. This one is shaped like a piece of Wookey Hole cheddar cheese," Bill stopped briefly before he said, "and after that Bruno should be able to see the cave opening."

I heard my Lady ask, "How do you know all of these rock formations are down there?"

Bill proudly stated, "With high tech machines, we can scan the underground cave system. We just cannot fit through it."

With a question in Lady's voice, she asked, "How will my Bruno know where to go?"

With that, I yelled as loud as I could possibly yell, "I'M DOWN HERE! I HEAR YOU ALL LOUD AND CLEAR! DO YOU ALL HEAR ME?"

I heard my voice say it over and over again and again. I waited and waited to hear any voices of hope back from Bill, Ava, and my Lady.

It was so silent. As I waited and waited, I looked over at the River Axe who had been with me from the start of my journey. I could hear the River Axe pushing against rocks as it formed new rocks. I thought, "I've never talked with River Axe before. It works hard to give Wookey Hole amazing rocks." I stopped thinking about me and I thought of River Axe. I said, "River Axe, you are so creative! You have done a great job with Wookey Hole, keep up the good work!" As I watched, the River pushed its waves up to me and said, "Thank you, Bruno!"

While smiling out at River Axe, I began to hear more

voices of hope from above! "Bruno, this is Lady. Are you okay?" she said with excitement in her voice. "I'm okay Lady, but I miss being in your garden and swing," I said as I thought back to what felt like so long ago. Bill said, "Bruno, all you have to do is follow these directions and I can get you out of there. Did you find the squiggly-lined cave wall?" I nodded my head and then stopped. I had to say something. Bill would never see my head through the cave ceiling or his cave floor, so I yelled back, "Yes, Bill, pleeeeease get me out of here!!!" Ava said, "Just follow my Bill's directions. You can do it!"

Bill repeated the directions for me one more time. "Swim through the low tunnel and past the large, spiky hedgehog rock. Then, you will see the rock that looks like a piece of Wookey Hole cheddar cheese in front of you. You have to climb over this one. After all of that you should see an opening to come out of," Bill said calmly.

I thought about everything Bill told me. I am good at following my nose, but I couldn't use my nose in the water. I had to trust Bill. I knew Bill was brilliant. I had to remember all these directions. I started with a little worry in my belly that got bigger and bigger that it made my head spin around again, just like it had when I went through the deep dark hole. I started to pull on my backpack straps. I wanted to open it to get my thinking stone but there was no need to get my backpack tools wet. There were stones all around me. I smiled and picked up a smooth cave rock to hold. I rubbed it and it worked just like the thinking stone in my backpack.

Bill and Lady called back to me. Bill gave me the directions again until I was able to say them all back to him in order. Bill yelled in his echo, "YOU CAN DO THIS, BRUNO. I believe in you." Lady yelled in her echo, "DON'T GIVE UP, BRUNO. I need you." Ava yelled in her echo, "KEEP ON TRYING, BRUNO. I will see you soon."

I had a big smile on my face. Even River Axe smiled back at me. I gave my Wookey Hole thinking stone a squeeze in my hand so I could say goodbye to it and I placed it right where I picked it up. I was feeling as brave as I was when I started my journey through the meadow. When I started, I didn't have a plan. Back then, I was looking for just one friend.

Filled with the love of my new friends, I took a breath in and let it out as I thought about how happy I would be when I saw them again. I tightened my goggles. After that, I picked up my helmet and put it on carefully. I pulled out the super-strong underwater glue that Ava tucked under the yellow ribbon tied around my waist and sealed my helmet back up. Then, I turned the valve on for my oxygen.

As I got ready to dive back into the water, but not without stopping to smile. Bill gave me a plan and I believed it was going to work!

I dove back into a calmer River Axe. It didn't try pushing me from side to side. Maybe it heard Bill's directions, too and wanted to help me get back to my friends.

I swam on, passing more fish. I nodded as I passed by. I still hadn't seen the kingfish's crown. He looked sad. I hoped he would find it soon. I didn't know what would happen to the underwater kingdom of fish if he didn't find it! I wished I could stop to help, but I had directions to follow so I swam on and on.

I was starting to get tired again when I came to the tunnel. Bill called it a low tunnel. It was a perfect fit for me! I swam straight through. Everything was cool now that I had a plan about how to get out of here. Things were starting to look better and better.

I found the first rock formation, the tunnel!

I looked at my circle pointer and it confirmed Bill's

directions to go straight ahead. Next, I had to find the spiky hedgehog rock. As I thought back to the real hedgehog, it reminded me of my super flips. I was feeling so happy about finding the first landmark that I took time to do a flip in the water! I thought if I did a perfect flip performance, maybe the spiky hedgehog rock would like it!

It was so easy flipping in the water that I did it over and over again! But there was one problem. I hadn't seen the spiky hedgehog rock. I was too busy doing my flips that I forgot about the directions so I swam back looking for the hedgehog rock.

I was starting to get worried when...

"OUCH!!!" The spiky hedgehog rock poked me!

Even though it hurt for three seconds, I was glad I found the spiky hedgehog rock.

I found the second rock! As I swam past the spiky hedgehog rock, I saw the biggest rock I had ever seen. I floated and stared at the rock that was shaped as Wookey Hole cheddar cheese!

I found the third rock, too! I had to get out of the water and start to climb. While I was glad I had my wetsuit, it was not going to make the climb easier if I was dripping with water! The Wookey Hole cheddar cheese rock was taller than Lady's thatched roof house! I knew it was going to be a big climb!

I put my helmet carefully into my backpack. I got my hands ready for a workout. I stretched my legs against the Wookey Hole cheddar cheese rock and started climbing, one leg at a time. I pushed my left leg up and then did the same with my right. It was harder to climb after being wet. I climbed and climbed. As I moved, I thought back to the Wookey Hole cheddar cheese Room. There was so much cheese there! This would have been a lot easier if it was real cheese. At least with real cheese, I could eat my way through!

There was no place to stop and rest along the way. The rock was huge! I wasn't going to let go because it was a straight drop back into River Axe! I wasn't going to give up! I had to stay focused!

I stopped climbing and closed my eyes. I thought back to Bill, Lady, and Ava's words. They said, "YOU CAN DO THIS! DON'T GIVE UP! KEEP ON TRYING!"

# Chapter 11

I opened my eyes with a smile on my face. With my friends supporting me through their words, I wasn't going to give up! I took a deep breath and held it for seven seconds. As I slowly let the air out, I said to myself, "I've got this! I believe in me!" I kept on climbing with one leg in front of another. I was getting so tired! I remembered what Bill said on the tour about not looking down on the bridge. I didn't mean to, but I looked back down from the cheese shaped rock! It was a long way down, but I had to keep going!

I climbed slowly, with all the power I had left in my

whole body. I wasn't going to give up! As I reached the top of the cheddar cheese rock, the yellow ribbon got stuck on the rock. I climbed over it and rubbed my eyes. The sun was trying to peek into the cave above me. I knew it was smiling at me!

I stretched out my hand into the sunlight! I finally made it out of the cave! I pushed with all of the energy left in my body. It was a struggle to crawl out. When I made it out of the cave, I fell to the ground and gave the grass a big kiss! I was back on green grass! I took my backpack off and started to roll in the grass. I heard it 'squeesh' back and forth with delight. I knew it was happy to see me, too.

A lot of things happened to me. I stopped rolling to replay the big moments in my head. I remembered feeling so sad and lonely in my meadow so far away. I also remember making up my mind to go on a journey to find just one friend. My trip started out rocky when the swan and hedgehog wouldn't even talk to me. I was polite to them even though I didn't understand why they wouldn't say one word to me, not even a, "Hi." One thing I do admit is that I scared the poor hedgehog, but I didn't mean to! And I can't forget the sheep that laughed at me! I probably turned bright red at the time. I make mistakes sometimes, but I'm not the only one that does, at least I hope I'm not! I don't like feeling embarrassed, even if it is just in front of a sheep.

I also met Bill and the cavers. He spoke to me, but not for long, at least not the first time we met. The best part came next! I met a real, true friend that loves to garden, cook, and teach me how to read and write. Just thinking about Lady makes me smile.

I smiled until I remembered how I got into all this. My Lady loves Wookey Hole, so I suggested that she go back for a visit. When my Lady was on her way out, I fell into her backpack with the weird straps. I thought it was super scary in her backpack until

I fell out of it into the cave. The cave was so much darker and scarier! I felt all alone. I was so lost until I met Ava, who was great company in the cave. We talked about Wookey Hole, Lady's home, and the yummy Wookey Hole cheddar cheese! I had to stop thinking about the cheese because it was making me more and more hungry.

I learned that my friends, Ava and Bill were close friends. They even worked together in the cave. Ava was so proud of her Bill. Then Ava taught me all about underwater caving. We both thought it was the only way out of the cave.

And just when I could have been saved by my Lady, I was washed away by the River Axe with its power! I was so glad there was an opening and voices of hope from Bill, Ava, and my Lady to help me make it out of Wookey Hole! I didn't see any of my friends! I started to feel the knot in my stomach, and it was getting bigger and bigger.

I wanted that feeling to go away, so I took my backpack off and rolled onto my back to tried to calm down with a tool, I call cloud dreaming. I saw clouds shaped like sheep. I even saw a cloud that reminded me of the spiky hedgehog. I kept looking for clouds that looked like the swan and Ava. Everything was going okay for a dark, cloudy day until I felt that first drop on my face. I thought to myself, "Really? More water? I just got out of the second watery cave under Wookey Hole!" For about three seconds, I forgot that I was in England. It rains a lot in England.

I grabbed my backpack and scurried to a dry spot under some rocks close by. I was going to try my best to stay dry. I looked around. I didn't see my Lady's house. I didn't see any of my friends either. I was in the middle of a field with tall grass and rocks. As the rain continued to pour down, I stopped and stared. I had never been here before! I took out my thinking stone and held it tightly, trying not to panic.

I thought and thought about it. Then, I suddenly knew just what to do. I searched for my magazine page. I stared at it for a long time. I loved all the pictures of Wookey Hole, but looking at the picture made me realize that the hole that I came out of was not Wookey Hole! As my eyes started to feel like they were going to pour out buckets of tears, I heard voices talking. I pulled those tears back up. There was no time to cry. I needed to find out where I was and how I was going to find my Lady!

Standing in the grass was a woman who was talking to two children. I heard her say, "We are going to have so much fun climbing down the hole and taking a short hike in the cave. That is why we practiced climbing outside yesterday in the daylight. You both will do a great job, I'm sure of it. Remember, it will be very dark inside the cave." As I listened, I agreed that caves are dark. I knew this from experience. I kept listening to gather more clues about where I was.

The woman kept talking to the children. She was laughing as she said, "This weather is also going to get us ready for the water inside the cave. That is why we have caving gear and lights. This is going to be so much fun. Welcome to Swildon's Hole!"

I couldn't help but ask, "Swildon's Hole??! What have you done with Wookey Hole?" The woman kept on walking and talking to the children. The boy said, "Mom, did you say something about Wookey Hole?" The woman shook her head no, but then the girl asked, "Mom, I heard it, too. Someone asked you what you did with Wookey Hole. What did you do with it, Mom?"

The woman laughed and turned to her son and daughter and said, "This is Swildon's Hole. We will climb down into it and walk in the water. It will be high in parts, so stay right with me."

That was all good advice, but I needed to know

where Wookey Hole was so, I kept listening, hoping the woman would say something about it to the children. I was glad the kids were at least able to hear me, even if the woman could not.

Then the woman started talking again to the kids as she pointed to a map on a rock. "Wookey Hole is over two miles from here and the caves do not connect. Wait...I know an old, old story that the Mendip Hills' Caving Club tells about Wookey Hole and Swildon's Hole. Would you like to hear it?"

The kids and I begged to hear it, yelling loudly, "Please, please, please." I stared at the woman. I didn't want to miss any part of a good story. I sat down beside the children in the tall, green grass. My ears perked up while I waited to hear the story. The kids stared at the woman waiting to hear the story, too.

She said, "There is a very old, old story called a

legend. A legend is a story that has been passed down from long ago. The Mendip Hills surround beautiful Somerset, England." As the woman spoke, she moved her arms from side to side to show how far away the caves were.

I didn't realize there was more than one cave. I had no idea where I was. I quickly took a deep breath in and out. I didn't want to miss a single word the woman said. I had to find my Lady and my new friends, Bill and Ava!

The woman told her kids and me, "The cavers talk about a small creature that will travel from far away. The creature will start at the beginning of Wookey Hole and swim through an underwater tunnel. It is very dark and scary down there. He will be a brave little soul and follow a path that only a few know exist. The creature will then need to squeeze through a teeny tiny opening for two and a half miles. This path will connect the two caves."

The kids' mouths opened wide with amazement and together they said, "Wow!" Then the boy said, "Do you think it will ever happen?" Then the girl chimed in saying, "Who would be that brave?"

The woman said, "It's just a legend. No one has ever been able to get through, but the Mendip Hills' Caving Club does want this dream to become reality."

I squealed with delight and yelled, "I did it! I made the dream come true! I did it! Yesssss! I am the brave creature!

The brother and sister jumped up and down, shouting, "Mom, the legend has come true! There is someone here saying so!" The boy and girl looked around, but they didn't see me. The woman hadn't heard me or seen me, but it didn't bother me as it did with the cavers in their shiny black suits because this time I made a legend come true! I was brave!

The mom shook her head no, put her hands on her hips, and said, "Kids, there is no way anyone can get through...." The woman suddenly stopped talking as we all turned to a loud noise coming towards us.

The noise we heard was a squeeshing sound in the grass. It was from Bill! He was running so fast through the fields. He came to find me.

I yelled, "Bill, where's my Lady?"

Bill slowed his running to catch his breath and replied, "Lady and Ava are at Wookey Hole. I'm glad to see you. As Bill caught his breath, he asked, "Did you have fun exploring?"

The woman looked at Bill. Then she looked all around. She asked Bill, "Who are you talking to? My kids and I haven't even been inside of Swildon's Hole yet."

Bill said, "I'm talking to my friend, Bruno. He took a journey through Wookey Hole and has just come out of Swildon's Hole."

With her mouth open wide, the mom looked on as I climbed up the rock with the map on it. This is the same rock that the woman showed her kids! I put my hands on my hips and gave them a big grin. After all, I did make a legend come true.
It stopped raining and the sun came out to shine on all of us.

The boy and girl jumped for joy and yelled, "The legend has come true, Mom!"

# Chapter 12

The boy and girl continued to yell, "I'm going to go tell Dad what happened today!" And with that said, they both raced off as fast as they could go.

Bill and the woman spoke more about the Mendip Hills' Caving Club. She wanted to start spreading the news that the two caves had been brought together by a mouse! She quickly said goodbye to Bill and pulled out her cell phone to spread the news, while running to catch up with her kids.

"We better get back to Wookey Hole. Lady and Ava are waiting for us," Bill said.

I agreed and Bill picked me up and put me in his shirt pocket. As Bill carried me I felt, not only proud but tall for a mouse. We walked and talked in the sunlight all the way to Wookey Hole. I could tell it was really Wookey Hole by the picture from my magazine page that I memorized. Wookey Hole is amazing!

There were so many people at Wookey Hole. I looked through the crowd to find my Lady. Bill continued to watch for Lady and Ava, too. Bill put his hands over his ears. There was so much noise from everyone talking at once. I could tell that Bill felt uncomfortable with all this noise. He needed it to stop. I was searching the crowd for my Lady and Ava. When I began to give up and feel sad, I heard a very kind voice that I heard before. That voice liked to garden. That voice liked opera music. That voice taught me how to read and write. That voice liked me! It was MY LADY!!!!! I jumped out of Bill's shirt pocket and landed onto my Lady's shoulder! I hugged her over and over again! My Lady gave me so many smushy kisses!

I looked at my Lady. She was smiling from ear to ear! She wanted to know everything about my great journey underwater, but she could tell that I was tired. All I wanted was to be right where I was, right by her side. She gave me a big hug and I curled up in her hand, right where I belonged. After a few seconds, I climbed onto my Lady's shoulder so I could see everything that was going on at Wookey Hole.

I looked over at Ava. She was wearing my Lady's dark sunglasses. I think they looked good on her! Ava flapped her wings close to Bill to muffle the sound of the crowd. As I watched Ava stay close to Bill, I realized that this was probably the first time she ever left her home at Wookey Hole.

I looked back at Bill. I knew he was relieved that we found my Lady and Ava, but there was something different about him. There was a smile on his face. I hadn't seen this before, and it was a good look on him. I was so proud of how he gave me directions to get out of Wookey Hole and came to my rescue. Bill is brilliant!

As I looked all around, I noticed that there were a lot of people at Wookey Hole. There were cavers in red caving suits and some in black shiny wetsuits, just like me. Everyone was talking over each other making my head start to hurt when all of a sudden, everyone stopped talking. I looked at people and they were staring at the sky. I gazed up to see an incredible sight! I blinked my eyes five times. It was a huge, red and yellow balloon! I never saw a balloon that big before! All I could say was, "Wow!" My Lady, Bill, and Ava were staring at the sky, too. Lady told me it was a hot air balloon.

People started pointing to the sky as the balloon started to come down. I saw a basket with a man standing inside of it. The hot air balloon kept floating downwards until it reached the ground. The man opened the basket door, walked right over to Bill, and asked, "What is going on here?" The crowd was completely silent as they listened.

Bill took the question without hesitation and explained how I went on a wild adventure through Wookey Hole that led me out at Swildon's Hole. The path that I took connected both caves. The man looked at Bill seriously and continued, "Can you prove this?" Bill smiled and said, "There is a yellow ribbon that starts in the deep, dark pond in Wookey Hole that stretches all the way through to the opening at Swildon's Hole." Bill pointed to me for the next part. "Just like the other cavers, I couldn't get through such a small opening, but I gave the directions to my mouse friend, Bruno, so he could get through it."

The man looked at me and then looked at Bill. The crowd waited patiently to hear what he would say next.

"This is the discovery I've been waiting for!" said the man. He paused for ten seconds as he looked at Bill's tour guide vest and name badge, then kept talking, "So, Bill, you are a tour guide here at Wookey Hole?"

Bill proudly said, "Yes sir, I am. I love Wookey Hole. It is my favorite cave. I am a tour guide here and I like to go caving at Wookey Hole."

With a smile on his face, the man replied, "You used strategies and hard work. I'm impressed with how you figured all of this out. I would like to promote you to Wookey Hole Caving Boss. Congratulations, you are now in charge of the new excavation project!"

The man smiled and continued talking. You'll be spending a lot of time at Wookey Hole. I trust in your judgment, Bill. You pick your crew of cavers and let me know anything you need for this huge project. You are in charge."

The man reached his hand out to shake Bill's hand. Bill looked at the man's hand and tried to touch it, but just couldn't bring himself to do it. The man saw Bill's frustration and slowly rotated his hand and closed his fingers into a fist. Bill grinned and gave the man an air knuckle bump. The crowd cheered. Bill nodded his head and said, "Thank you, sir, I accept the job. I won't let you down."

I could see Ava beaming with delight as her wings flapped back and forth as if she was dancing with joy for her Bill. I knew she would help with the excavation project, whatever that was.

The man turned to my Lady and said, "Congratulations to you and your mouse. I would like to offer him a reward. How would you like me to reward Bruno for finding this amazing discovery that I dreamed about for so long?

Lady looked at me and said, "You did all the work, Bruno. What would you like?"

I thought and thought some more. I was with my friends. I was so happy to be with them. I thought to myself, "Where could I go to be with them even more?" Then, I scampered back up to my Lady's shoulder and whispered into her ear.

Lady said to the man, "Bruno would like to come through the Wookey Hole tour with me as any other tourist does so he can see everything."

The man shook Lady's hand, looked at me and said, "It's a deal. I hope you enjoy Wookey Hole as it transforms over time with Bill's excavation project. Bruno, thank you for making the legend a reality."

I smiled at the man. My Lady gave me another hug.

The man turned back to Bill and said, "Oh, Bill, after you have your crew of cavers, be sure to let me know all their names. Here is my card."

He then turned back to me, "As for you, Bruno, enjoy Wookey Hole." And with that, the man opened the gate to his red and yellow hot air balloon basket and stepped inside. I waved at him as he floated away. Later, Bill explained to us that the man was the owner of Wookey Hole.

The other cavers that Bill explored with came by. I wondered what they would say so I listened carefully as they each greeted him, "Congratulations, Bill! You've done it! We are sorry for the way we treated you. It was not okay. Will you forgive us?"

Bill looked at the three cavers and then said, "Thank you for apologizing. I accept. Let's move forward, starting today." They all nodded in agreement. Bill got air high-fives from each of them. All the other cavers lined up to congratulate Bill, as well.

Bill climbed onto a rock and said in a loud voice, "I will need a lot of help to excavate this area and to connect Wookey Hole to Swildon's Hole. It will be a big job. I know exactly the way we need to go to get this done. Raise your hand if you want to help me make this excavation project come true."

I looked at the crowd of cavers. Some of them were in black wetsuits and others in caving suits. They all had their hands raised. Ava's wings were in the air, too!

The crowd of cavers started chanting, over and over again, "Caving Boss, Bill! Caving Boss, Bill!" The cavers were all proud of him. Bill smiled just a little and waved at the crowd. Supportive Ava felt proud of her Bill as she hovered above Bill's head.

Bill continued to talk, "Go home and get some sleep. We will start tomorrow morning."

I could hear the cavers respond loudly, "Yes, sir." Talkative, smiling cavers started walking away, excited to begin the project with Bill.

Lady said, "Bill and Ava, we have to celebrate your new job! Bruno and I want you all to come to our house."

I thought, "Did I hear that right?" I couldn't believe that she said, "OUR house." My heart started pumping even faster with delight!

Bill and Ava had never been to a party before. Ava nodded her head yes to Bill. Bill accepted, too.

Even though it was right beside Wookey Hole, my Lady drove Bill, Ava, and I to the bakery. They were open late for sweet treats.

As Ava held onto the weird straps of Lady's backpack, hanging upside down, she yelled to Lady, "No nuts, please! They get stuck in my teeth." My Lady nodded as she walked into the store. Ava, Bill, and I waited in the car wondering what my Lady would get for our party. I didn't tell anyone, but I had never been to a party before either. I was super excited!

Bill was busy planning by writing notes in a notebook. He made a list of all the tools he would need to excavate. He also made a list of jobs to do and put them in order. Ava and I watched the sunset. It was a beautiful orange color. Time passed quickly as it always does with friends. My Lady returned from the store with boxes that she put in the trunk of the car. She smiled as she looked at each of us and gave me another welcome home hug. As she drove, she looked at me sitting on her dashboard with love in her eyes and said, "I'm so proud of you, Bruno." I smiled back as my tail curved up into a heart and I simply said, "I couldn't have done any of this without help from my friends."

Bill, Ava, and my Lady agreed. Everyone needs friends in their life.

When we arrived at our thatched roof house, my Lady pulled out all the packages of treats. She let Ava and Bill carry red and yellow balloons inside. I got to sit on top of my Lady's zipped up backpack with the weird straps, but this time I didn't fall inside of it!

Lady put yellow and red streamers all around the Great Room. As we sat down in the Great Room, Ava flew around looking at all the pictures on the wall of Wookey Hole and other sweet memories. My Lady talked about her grandfather and her love of Wookey Hole. We each shared special memories of Wookey Hole. And then my Lady thought of a great idea! We took a picture of all of us using her selfie stick. It was a great picture! She was going to get it printed and framed so we would become part of the wall of great memories!

As we sat, we started to talk about our favorite part of the great adventure. According to Bill, the best part was giving me directions through the watery cave under Wookey Hole. This led to the discovery of the exit. As Bill said the word, discovery, he looked up as his eyes opened wider. We all turned and looked up, but all we could see was the ceiling of Lady's thatch roof house. I think Bill saw something we didn't see. He stopped talking and continued to look up.

Ava shared about how much she enjoyed having me come to visit her at Wookey Hole. Because of how I got there, I didn't really think it was a visit, but there was no way I was going to take that smile off her face, so I didn't say a word and I just smiled.

When it was my Lady's turn, she shared so many favorite moments; meeting me in the garden, finding me at Wookey Hole, and of course, the party.

As I looked around and thought of my amazing adventure, I loved every moment of it. I know that sounds strange when I had so many ups and downs along the way, but if I didn't have downs, how could I know how good the ups were? I smiled as I thought about my adventures and looked at my three friends.

Lady turned on some opera music and Bill and I covered our ears. Ava put her wings over her ears, too. "Alright, I will change the music, my Lady said. Then she asked, "Bruno, do you have suggestions for the right celebration music?" Without hesitation, I raced to her cell phone and played music to dance to. Lady and Ava clapped for the music and I bowed. After all, I am a legend with great taste in music.

My Lady asked me to dance. I jumped up and down. I was so excited to have my dance partner back. She held me, as usual, carefully in her hand as we danced. I looked up at my Lady who was dancing with her eyes closed. I saw Ava swaying to the music in flight when suddenly she stopped

dancing! She flew right to Bill! I looked over at Bill.
He was staring at my Lady and me. I watched him
watch us. The more my Lady and I danced, the
bigger Bill's eyes got, but he had a scared look
on his face, not a happy look. Before I could say
anything to my Lady about my worries for Bill, I
heard Ava ask, "Bill do you want to dance with
me?" As Bill slowly nodded, the smile on his face
grew. His eyes changed from scared eyes to happy
eyes. With Ava still flying around Bill and moving
with the music, he started dancing just like me on my
journey to find my Lady. He moved his head back
and forth. He moved his arms from side to side. He
added three jumps to his dancing. "Wow, Bill is a
good dancer," I said. My Lady opened her eyes
and agreed with me. I kept watching my friends as
I continued dancing in my Lady's hand. I thought
about how I started out all alone, but through my
ups and downs, I found forever friends. I knew we
could do anything together!

I thought more and more about spending time with my three friends, my smile grew bigger and bigger. I didn't have any more big-sized problems, at least at this party and with my friends. I looked down at my feet. They agreed with me. In fact, they even looked smaller to me. We all danced more and more.

When we were all tired from dancing, we walked to my Lady's kitchen and sat at the round table to eat, well...except Ava. She continued to fly above Bill's chair. We all watched as my Lady opened the scrumptious treats. She held carefully in her hands an assortment of trays with many delicious things to try and placed them in the middle of the round table. We talked about each dessert and what we wanted to try. There were sugar-free blueberry tarts, gluten-free cupcakes in all different colors, and strawberry cheesecakes made with the famous Wookey Hole cheddar cheese! As we raised our water glasses to toast to our friendship and our great adventure to find each other, I stopped to say, "I'm so happy that you are all my friends. Everything is so much sweeter with all of you in my life." I could feel a happy tear come down my face and I let it roll right down past my big smile. Altogether, we all said, "Cheers! Friends forever!" We clinked our water glasses together and started to dig into the sweet treats.

As I watched and listened to my three friends talk, I found myself daydreaming once again as I wondered what my next adventure would be. One thing I knew for sure was that I made great friends. This had been an amazing adventure! But what we have is more than that so I thought and thought. And then a brilliant idea came to me! With my pointer finger raised into the air, I announced to all, "I will call this *the friendship adventure!*"

# Meet the Author

Q: What is your name?

A: My name is Carole G. Barton.


Q: Who was the most influential person in your life when you were growing up?

A: Growing up, the person who influenced me the most was my mom.

Q: How did your mom influence you?

A: My mom was a teacher and I wanted to be just like her. As a child, I was shy in large group settings and that led me to believe that I wouldn't be a good teacher. I later learned that as a speech therapist, I could work with a small group of students to encourage them to become better communicators. Thanks to the impact my mom made on my life, I have been working as a speech therapist for over 25 years.

Q: What do you like to write about?

A: I love writing about real places all over the world, kindness, and problem-solving!

Q: How do you use children's books in your life as a teacher?

A: I use children's books to teach my speech therapy students about friendship, problem-solving, emotional intelligence, social skills, and speech.

Q: How does being a speech therapist make you a better writer?

A: The impact reading makes in my students' lives acts as a constant reminder of the impact my mom made in her own life using literature. It was this constant reminder that inspired me to follow my dream of becoming an author!

Q: Will Bruno and his friends be in your next story?

A: Yes, Bruno and his friends will continue to go on fun adventures together. The Friendship Adventure is the first book in my brand new children's book series, Bruno's Friendship Chronicles™. I plan to write many more adventures over the years!

Q: What is the most valuable thing you've learned as an author that you can share with your readers?

A: The most valuable thing I've learned in my journey as a children's book author is that I can do anything that I commit to doing. So, my advice to anyone reading this is to follow your dreams! You can do anything you commit to doing, too. The important thing is to spread kindness along the way!

Made in the USA
Columbia, SC
30 January 2021